EMPERORS & ASSASSINS

DB BRAY

with WAHIDA CLARK

Emperors & Assassins

Wahida Clark Presents Publishing
60 Evergreen Place
Suite 904A
East Orange, New Jersey 07018
1(866) 910-6920
www.wclarkpublishing.com

Library of Congress Cataloging-In-Publication Data:

EMPERORS & ASSASSINS
ISBN 978-1-954161-09-2 paperback
978-1-954161-10-8 epub
978-1-954161-11-5 Audiobook

LCCN: 2020943114
1. Fantasy 2. Urban life 3. Crime 4. Romance 5. Fast life 6. Street Literature

Cover design and layout by Nuance Art, LLC
Book design by www.artdiggs.com
Editorial Team: Natalie Sade and Phillip Smith
Printed in United States

EMPERORS & ASSASSINS

Prologue

The people in the world of Dellos needed a hero.
An explosive light resonating in the grim darkness, a gift
from the god's sent to fight tyranny and oppression . . .

Viridius wished he could wipe the sweat from his face, but he knew his father would exploit the slightest inattention. Flicking his shield towards his father, he aimed a quick thrust at his foot. His timing was perfect, his father brought his shield down, punching the sharp sword at his son's face. Viridius slammed his shield up into his Rotix's wrist, sending his sword spinning away. Knowing Rotix Vispanius was never disarmed, Viridius slashed, feinting for his father's face, and used his pommel to pull Rotix's shield out of position, cannoning his shield rim into his father's chest. Viridius wasn't done, darting in low under the cover of his shield his fired a thrust for his father's throat.

Rotix's foot snapped out connecting Viridius' face. At fourteen he could best most grown men easily but his father was not most men. The chocolate hue of his skin marked him as a descendents the Ansawari, one of the most ancient civilizations on Dellos. Once over forty tribes had strode the continent, many no longer remained. Only the Iyrjet, the Ebedja, the Uhmara, the Grio, the Fahlbe, Dongla and Gobo remained. The rest called themselves Tramonians who shared a hue, and a history, but had been conquered and colonized by waves of invaders from the sea to the west.

"You must be faster! We are the of the, Gobo! We heirs of the Answari! We are the tip of the spear and we must by our the blood of our ancestors always be harder and sharper than any fighters in Wolfrya!" Viridius picked himself up, striking a ready stance hoping his shield and helmet hid his expression.

"He almost had you," Palix said, but his father would have none of it. Viridius slammed his sword on the rim of his shield letting his father know he was ready...hopefully avoiding one of his Rotix's famous speeches. They would all be ancestors by the time his father finished. Viridius eyed his brother over his shield rim, mouthing in time with his father, hiding his smirk.

"Long before Emperor Fabian, the Ansawari, ruled from the Lava Lands to the the plains north of Iceport. It was our ancestors who taught the Trammonian civilization!" Rotix leapt at Viridius, having managed to retrieve his sword without his son ever noticing, cutting hard and fast, two low strikes, one high, a middle strike, then another low. Viridius grunted working his shield to keep his father's flurry of blows, but his father hadn't even even stopped his speech.

"There were seven main tribes among our people, led by their Sarauniya, a warrior queen and an Eparch, selected by the elders." Viridius kept his shoulders square to his father, seeking to weather his attacks with the same aplomb he managed to weather his father's constant lessons on loyalty, duty and their lineage. Their line of Imperial Prefects was as old as the empire itself.

His father hammered away still speaking,

"When the beast men came seeking their slaves, we were there to meet them with steel and determination! Viridius, had found his father's rhythm, swatting his sword aside he struck, faking high. But his father was ready for his tricks, and smothered Viridius with his shield.

Trained for the Wolfryan shield wall he knew he could not step back, he could not step aside, to do so would expose his shield brothers around him.

"Who do you think was the point of that spear?!" His father bellowed.

"Ta Gobo!" Viridius shouted in unison with his brother Palix, widening his stance and crouching lower into the immense pressure of his father's attack.

"Have you ever seen a Ba boy?" His father roared like the leonine beast men of the accursed lava lands.

"Nine feet tall, fangs sharp as swords and claws to match, five times as strong as the strongest man! It was the Gobo who met them! WHO ARE YOU?" Viridius shifted his weight and unbalanced Rotix, leaving his father hyperextended, as his son struck around his shield aiming for his armpit.

"I AM VIRIDIUS VISPANIUS, I AM A WEAPON OF WOLFRYA, I AM THE POINT OF THE SPEAR!" he roared sensing his impending victory. But his father was too fast, moving like wind whipped water, parrying Viridius' attack and launching his own.

"Wrong," his father said softly launching a now offensive flurry forcing Viridius to shelter behind his shield to fend away lightning cuts, and serpentine thrusts interspersed with liberal bashes of his shield. The technique was old as the ice. Wa-tahtib was passed down by the Gobo from father to son's. As boys he and Palix had been given sticks and been instructed in it's ways. At first they thought it and odd dance until their lessons progressed. The shield was never just for defense and could break a skull or shatter ribs as easily as the sword can cut.

"You are a son of the Gobo, knights of the Ansawari. All tribes of the Ansawari mastered the bow, sword, axe and spear, but the Gobo mastered all these, and the horse. When we fought the Ba we would form up two riders knee to knee, then three, then four and so on, until a we were formed like the point of a mighty spear and we would slice through enemy line like a spear point through a gap in armor!"

As if to punctuate his statement Rotix shoved aside his defenses, hit point on target for a kill, but Viridius flowed around the attack, and launched a storm of blows of his own. His father was forced back a step but his tirade did not falter.

"From the time of Emperor Fabian we have served Wolfrya, not the emperor do you know why? Do you know where you loyalties lie?" Rotix hissed.

The questions unbalanced Viridius,this is not part of the normal speech, and he lost his focus for a split second, all his father needed to recover. Viridius had never spent much time pondering his ancestry. For three hundred years his forefathers had been prefects of Wolfrya, it was what it meant to be of his line. Vispanius hammered with his shield as father continued.

"The dream of empire feed on blood son. Our blood. The elders of the Gobo, seeking to prevent war, sent their princes to serve as bodyguards to the emperor. Hostages, sword and shield all at the same time. Old emperor Fabian knew our value, and this is why rather than fight us he made us titles. But no matter how much gold inlay you lavish, or how many jewels you adorn it with, a sword is still a weapon, it's still expendable...Wolfryian swords cut both ways." His father strode away, leaving him feeling confused.

CHAPTER

Viridius Vispanius wasn't their hero; never would be. With a deep sigh, he yanked the head of his axe out of the skull in front of him and wiped the blood and brain matter across his leather breeches. Battle exhausts everyone, even the most battle-hardened. And for those who survive, it's a curse. A curse that can only be cured by dying in the next battle. But Viridius was never that lucky.

He was a mercenary in Batopia, a lawless land in the north, a cesspool of the worst kind—his kind. He had been hiding in the north for almost a year, longing for a way to get back to his old life.

I hate Wolfryian raiding parties, he thought.

A silky black crow squawked behind him, cracking the still air. He turned his neck slightly and watched the bird fly over his shoulder, its white droppings splattering against his leather pauldrons as it climbed higher into the sky.

Damn Dellosian crows—worthless animals, he thought, smearing the white droppings off his armor. *By the gods, I hate this damn place.*

He spat a stream of tobacco juice from between his pursed lips, the majority of it hitting the dead body. The sun overhead beamed down on his bald head as the beads of sweat slowly dripped off the stubble on his chin. His skin was dark, the battle scars across his chest taut and thick.

Glancing at the bodies around him, Viridius snorted and then took a long pull off of his canteen. The field lay littered with the dead and those who would be joining them shortly.

He slammed his ax head into the wet ground and leveraged himself up with a loud sigh, his joints popping and creaking an unwelcome sound. He walked toward the woods on the far side of the blood-drenched clearing and took to the grim task of dispatching the unlucky mercenaries still alive. He sawed their throats like a woodsman felling a tree.

He drowned out the moans and gasps they made with a low whistle as his knife slid across their throats. After finishing, he walked over the threshold of the woods with his ax swung over his shoulder. Glancing into the sky for any birds large enough to swoop down on him for an easy dinner, he misstepped and stumbled over a tree root. He struggled to his feet and swiped the palm of his hand over his sweat-drenched face, and then turned around.

He cleared his throat and spat. *Damn, I really hate this place.*

With a quick glance over his shoulder, he grabbed his pack and walked out onto the road leading to the village of Pistoryum. The dust swirled around his ankles as he walked, the smell of blood heavy on his leather armor as he approached the gate.

He stayed in the shadows as he meandered his way to the closest bar in the village. The few coins he managed to take off the dead jingled in the pouch hanging from his belt. He slipped into the bar, the patrons barely noticing his hulking frame.

He wasn't handsome by Wolfryian standards, but he would do as a bed warmer in Batopia. His most noticeable feature was his eyes, one dark green, the other a smoky hazel.

He sat down on a rickety bar stool and ordered a mug of ale with a mutton pie. He ate quietly, and after he finished, he pounded his battle-scarred fist on the table and looked around.

Where's that barmaid? He took another pull on the brittle wooden lip of his mug. *Haven't got all day. I need another drink.*

He stared at the man next to him in disgust as he watched him shovel more gruel into his mouth. Shaking his head, Viridius glanced at the faces around him.

Never can be too careful.

Among the scattered wooden tables, men and women played different card games. Viridius glanced up in time to see a man fall out of his chair, a knife buried to the hilt in his throat. The ace of spades tumbled from the cuff of the gambler's sleeve.

Stupid, really stupid. Never keep an ace up your sleeve. It's too obvious.

The guards dragged the dead man through the bar, his blood leaking onto the boards. They pushed the patrons walking in front of them out of the way as they worked their way to the cheap door. Then they launched the body out into the street for the feral dogs to finish what the gamblers had begun.

Viridius glanced up as another brawl erupted over a prostitute behind him. He glanced over his shoulder and watched the man taking the worst of the beating yank a knife from his belt.

Viridius stared at the knife. *Oh, that's not—*

A guard standing nearby swung his sword down and cut off the attacker's hand, the knife clattering harmlessly on the floor as the man screeched, staring at his bloody knob. The guard yanked the man's head back from behind and ran his blade through his back. The bloody tip of the blade exploded through the man's sternum, splattering blood over Viridius's boots.

Ah, fuck me.

"Down, boss," the guard said, pointing to the other man as he sheathed his sword.

The local watering hole was called The Blade, the local mercenary hangout. But it was more of a shanty than an actual functional tavern. The rotting wood on the exterior of the building allowed the cold wind to blow through the cracks, chilling its patrons to the bone.

The prostitutes above him leaned over the railing and talked among themselves. For a good time with them it was only a few coins, and Viridius snickered as he heard the loud moans from behind the slim wooden doors on his left.

He pulled his hood closer to his face, flexing his arthritic fingers as he spun a coin on the table. Although he didn't stick out in the tavern among the other patrons, he was still an imposing figure, his shoulders tight around his dirty, stained blue tunic.

His eyes scanned the bar, trying to spot an ale someone left unattended. Two men argued beside him about the Wolfryian emperor and his iron grip on the throne.

He hiccuped and thought. *Oh, if they only knew.*

One of the patrons shoved the other, escalating the argument. Viridius used the distraction to pull both mugs over to him. He drained them, burped, and then pushed them back.

Then he pushed himself off the stool, stumbled over to an empty table, and sat down. He squinted at a young boy as he ambled over with a pitiful look, grimy hand out. Viridius stared at him, then pushed him to the ground with his large palm. With a drunken chuckle, he snatched a mug of ale as it passed by.

The server turned around and said, "That's fa' somebody else!"

Like I care.

After a long swig, he burped again and then flipped a gold coin onto her serving plate. He pushed her and said, "More . . . now."

He glanced at his feet and scooped the ragged boy off the ground. He tossed him onto the opposite bench with a flick of his wrist. Using his thick index finger, he slid the mug of ale across the table to see what the boy would do. Staring at it, the boy licked his lips and reached for it like quicksilver.

Viridius yanked the mug back. "Tsk tsk tsk."

He pulled one of his last silver coins from his breast pocket. "Spirits will take your pain away for a moment, boy, but silver . . ." Effortlessly, he rolled the coin over his knuckles and stared into the boy's soft brown eyes. "This will haunt your nightmares no matter how much of it you have. It consumes my soul. Now, begone," he said, flipping him the coin. The corner of his lip upturned in a half smile.

The boy gave him a toothless grin and vanished.

Damn shame he won't live through the winter. Actually, none of these poor bastards are going to make it. He looked around at the smiling faces. *Never enough food to go around, only flesh.*

A prostitute caught his stare and walked over to his table. She picked up the coin he had been spinning and pocketed it.

"Fancy a ride? I'm better than most in here," she said, standing over him as she ran her calloused fingers over his scalp

"Not interested. Now, leave me to my drink," he said, staring straight ahead.

She leaned in closer and placed his hand on her breast. "Now, what do you think?"

On second thought . . .

He smiled and stood up, his legs wobbling. She took his hand and led him to a room. Walking through the doorway, she slipped out of her dress and sat down in the flea-ridden bed. She waved him over with her dirty index finger. He walked over to her, towering above her as she unbuttoned his pants. He pulled his tunic over his head and lay beside her.

Her fingers and mouth found every ache on his chiseled body. She heard him groan as she slowly started to ride him. She leaned back and hooked her arm around his neck. Viridius put his hands on her waist, and when he ejaculated, he wiped the sweat from his brow.

With a deep sigh, he rolled over and fell asleep for a few hours. When he woke up, he pulled his pants back on at the edge of the bed.

"You're right. That was better than most," he said, putting on his filthy tunic.

He walked to the door and left one gold coin on the dresser. He exited the room and sat back down at his table, peering at the other tables in the smoky room. Seeing nothing, he drank several more mugs of ale over the next few hours until the purse swinging from his side was empty.

Brooding about his misfortunes, he cracked his knuckles, thinking of when he would get his revenge on Emperor Octavius. *Fuckin' worthless bastard.*

Finally, his head dropped onto the table, and he passed out. A lone figure sat tucked away in the shadows of the tavern, wearing a forest-green cloak with a fur-lined hood. He had been watching Viridius drink, patiently waiting for his opportunity. Viridius should have been paying closer attention. He had too many enemies.

The silent figure sipped his mug of ale every few minutes and glanced around, trying to blend in with the shadows. As he scanned the faces, he noticed that no one seemed to see him sitting by himself as he tapped his long, thin fingers on the table. Silently, he approached Viridius from behind, carrying a large bucket.

The cold water he dropped on Viridius's head had the desired effect he wanted. Like lightning, Viridius rose from the bench and drew his sword from its worn scabbard. His legs wobbled for a moment, and then he bent over and vomited.

Ach . . . yellow bile. Should have eaten something other than the mutton pie. I never drink. I should have known better. What the hell happened, and why am I all wet?

He wiped the back his sleeve across his mouth to clear the bile off his face and then spit the remainder out of his mouth. He patted himself down and looked around, his body swaying with every hiccup. After his last hiccup, he felt his wet pants and squinted through the smoky atmosphere. He blinked the smoke out of his eyes and sat back down. He returned his sword to its sheath and stared at the man in front of him with mild amusement.

"Who are you supposed to be?" he asked, eyebrow raised.

The cloaked man sat down across from him and said, "I am the breeze rolling through the grass, the salt in the ocean, and the key to unlocking your miserable existence." He glanced around to make sure they weren't overheard and said, "Unless you like living like a pig in this cesspool."

With a snort, Viridius picked up his empty mug and raised it in his direction. "And I thought I was drunk because you definitely ain't rolling through my grass. Body parts ain't right. And I hate salt. Oh, how I hate the taste of salt. Now, you called my tavern a cesspool." He slammed his knife into the gnarled wood. "Be careful with your words, *friend*. You may offend me."

After a moment of silence, Viridius lit his pipe, pressing two fingers over the embers.

The stranger continued. "I am—"

Viridius muttered as he puffed, "Pissing me off. Now, I didn't tell you to fuckin' sit or ask you to. So, fuck off and leave me to my drinking."

"I am—"

Viridius glanced up again, his eyes leveling with the stranger's. He couldn't get a good look at his features because his hood was pulled as tight as his own. A wisp of smoke came from under Viridius's hood. "Perhaps you didn't hear me the first time. *Fuck off!*"

The other patrons quieted down to see if the yelling would escalate into a brawl. Disappointed, they went back to their drinks. The man made eye contact with Viridius again and dropped a leather purse onto the table.

"I'm looking for an old friend. Perhaps you have seen him," he said.

"Nah, don't think I have," Viridius said, cleaning the brown tobacco stains in his pipe.

"His name is Viridius Vispanius, former prefect to Emperor Tiberius of Wolfryia. Have I found him?"

Only for a moment did Viridius's eyes betray him from under his hood. He drew a sharp breath, and his body stiffened.

How does he know? I need to remain calm and not kill him. Be tough to explain it.

His eyes darted around the room, searching for a trap or any other men intent on killing him. Viridius's hand crept to the bone-handled knife on his left side, but at the last moment, he pulled it away.

While Viridius stared around the room, the stranger moved the large coin purse in front of him. Viridius eyed the purse and licked his lips, his greed taking over. He stared at the bag.

"If I'm the Prefect Viridius Vispanius you're looking for, it will depend on how many coins are in here. And who the hell are you—besides an annoying prick," he muttered.

The man ignored his insult. "There are five hundred coins in there." The stranger pulled his hood back and smiled wide.

Viridius's eyes bulged wide before he snatched his knife from its sheath. "Gius Flavius. You got a lotta nerve coming here after what you did."

Viridius removed his hood, then slammed the knife into the table. He slowly removed his other knives and placed them on the table, a cold, dead look in his eyes. "Give me one good reason why I shouldn't kill you right now."

"Easy, old man. Just listen to what I have to say, then kill me."

Viridius took a deep breath, looked at the purse, and then felt his own. "All right, I'm listening," he said, pushing his back against the booth he was sitting in.

Gius nodded at the purse, and Viridius glanced at it, his lips tight. He picked it up and glanced inside and then dropped it in disgust. Rubbing his fingertips with a frown, he stared at Gius.

"I thought you knew better than to give me Wolfryian gold. I wouldn't spend this if it was the last currency to buy ale and whores with," Viridius said, throwing the purse back in front of Gius, readying himself to leave the table.

"Don't be an idiot. There's plenty more where that came from. It all spends the same," Gius said, spinning a coin on the table. "Besides, I'm paying you to listen."

Viridius paused, sat back down, and lit his pipe again. "All right, I'll play along. What do you want, Gius?"

Gius took a long sip of his ale and then said, "I want you to kill Emperor Octavius."

Viridius coughed as the smoke left his lungs. He leaned forward and laughed until he had trouble drawing his breath.

"Ha. You always were a dreamer, Gius. Even if you could get to him, Asinius would make sure whoever assassinated him would suffer greatly before he gave them the gift of death," he said.

"Octavius isn't untouchable, Viridius. We got his father, and now the Rebellium needs your help. You were, at one point, one of the best warriors in Dellos before you became prefect. Hell, you killed more men than Jonas, the headman." Gius cleared his throat and leaned in to deliver the last of his message. "And the reason I came out of hiding was to ask you personally."

"Been rehearsing that speech, haven't you? Octavius ain't a threat. He's just another emperor. Besides, I hear that disgusting fat boy-king is sitting in luxury being fed grapes by naked boys," Viridius said.

Gius sighed. "What do we need to give you for your help then?" he asked.

"The world," Viridius mumbled, picking dirt from under his nails.

Gius shook his head and tapped his chin. Without a word, he grabbed Viridius by the back of the neck and with a quick pull, slammed his head onto the table. Knocked unconscious, Viridius fell off the bench.

Gius picked up the coin purse from the table, stooped down, and slung Viridius over his shoulder. Their server came up, holding a fresh mug of ale as he walked away from the table.

"He won't be needing it, my dear, but I do," Gius said, taking the mug.

"Hey, who's gonna pay fa' that?" she asked in her northern accent.

He slipped two gold coins into her calloused hand and closed it. "I will. And you never saw us, right?"

"All right, ya lardship, as you wish," she said, moving on.

The other patrons didn't notice or care as Gius carried another drunk into the blistering cold. The wind, hail, and freezing rain hit him in the face as he pushed the tavern door open. Trudging through ankle-deep snow, he carried Viridius to the room he was renting at the Sleeping Aardvark, an inn on the edge of town by the icy waters.

The Sleeping Aardvark wasn't glamorous. In fact, it was nasty. The sign hanging over the door had a black aardvark with red eyes painted on it, but the sign had seen better days. In its current state, it looked more like a fat rat than an aardvark.

The old black-and-white bordered Batopian flag flying over the door of the inn was torn and stained with blood from battles long forgotten, the bones of the dead soldiers who fought in them long since pulverized into dust.

The walls of the inn smelled like rotten fish, and the patrons didn't smell much better as they lounged around, void of emotion, most of them in a drunken or drugged stupor. Green algae oozed from the well in the courtyard, giving anyone who drank it terrible dysentery.

Gius had paid a month's rent with one gold coin and gave the innkeeper another one to keep his mouth shut. The innkeeper didn't bat an eye as he handed Gius his room key. There were plenty of criminals who came to the Sleeping Aardvark to disappear. It was nothing new.

The innkeeper stared over the rim of his round, metallic glasses as they entered. He was scribbling something in his ledger as Gius walked by.

Gius heard the innkeeper mutter to a patron, "I serve anyone, even Wolfr—"

Without looking at him, Gius cut him off and said, "Mind your business, old man, or I'll cut your tongue out."

Gius steadied himself as he walked up the stairs, straining with each step. Each stair creaked under their combined weight as he neared the top. Stepping onto the top board, it splintered into three pieces. He lost his balance and threw Viridius onto the landing with a strained grunt. As his ankle twisted, he heard his big toe snap. Soft curses escaped his lips as he bent down and grabbed his ankle.

He put as much weight as he could on it as he stumbled down the hallway. He fell into the wall several times but managed to drag Viridius by the arm to his room. "Oh, you fat, drunk bastard," he muttered.

As they cleared the door, Viridius rolled face-first onto the floor. Letting out a heavy sigh, Gius sat down on the lumpy bed and pulled his boots off, favoring his sprained ankle. He knew he had no right to ask for Viridius's help. The past physical and mental pain they both suffered were enough for any man to endure.

All the politicians, army commanders, and merchants in Wolfryia who associated with Octavius wanted him dead for the part they believed he played in Tiberius's death. Few, if any, of the politicians left opposed the newly minted emperor. Viridius had failed in his duty to protect Tiberius, something his son would never forget.

Tiberius, Octavius's father, was more prone to exterminating other races than his son was. The peasants called him "Clockwork," because his penchant for violence was as reliable as the continuous tick of a clock. Viridius's failure carried an automatic death sentence, and Octavius wanted the debt paid in full.

A plan had been hatched by the Rebellium council for Gius to recruit Viridius and have him assassinate the emperor in Iceport. It was a suicide mission, no doubt, but only a few men in Dellos could pull it off and maybe survive. Gius didn't know how he was going to get Viridius on board, but he had no other choice. Octavius had to die to restore order to the world.

Either Viridius joined the Rebellium, or Gius would kill him and protect the plan. It was always about the plan. But the one absolute Gius knew in the equation was Viridius would kill anyone if the price was right.

He knew killing people never really bothered Viridius. If people were innocent, he still killed them, only faster. A target was a target. It didn't matter the age, gender, or occupation, nor did he care. Princes to paupers, he had killed them all as if he were gutting a fish to eat.

A man who felt wronged like he did was doomed to die alone, as if he were needed to serve a purpose . . . a valiant purpose. Gius wanted to make sure if Viridius did die, it would be for that greater purpose . . . the Rebellium.

CHAPTER

Iceport, the capital city of the Kingdom of Wolfryia, was on the east coast of Dellos, where the crossroads of the kingdoms met. It was the largest city in the world, mightier than all the southern tribal tent cities, the only free people left who opposed the Wolfryian aristocracy.

Emperor Octavius Victorus stared at his young slave as he poured Tramonian wine into his empty lead-lined goblet. The emperor's taste for other wines had diminished over the years because of his constant consumption. He always wanted to appear more refined than he actually was, but even if he were refined, it wouldn't have shown in his daily life.

The emperor's wine was imported from the Kingdom of Tramonia far to the west on the opposite coast. The wine was only produced in Sorra, the capital city rivaling Iceport in size and commerce. The king of Tramonia could only sell his potent exported commodity to Emperor Octavius by royal decree, a fact that didn't sit well with King Aksutamoon of Sorra, his bitter rival.

Tears of Tramonia was the most expensive wine in Dellos because its cost caused the poor men of the world to cry. Only the emperor could afford to drink, anyway. The wine fetched a huge price on the black market, and most of the bandits and highwaymen who went after the merchants carrying it were Warlord Three Toes' men from Batopia— ruthless mercenaries who thrived on hijacking goods.

King Aksutamoon disappeared recently along with his latest shipment that he was hand delivering after the latest shipment had been hijacked. It was rumored he disappeared in Drathia, a no-man's-land south of Batopia.

Octavius's slave's clammy palm slipped on the wine handle as he poured the wine in front of him. The wine splashed across the emperor's forearm and stained his white sash inlaid with gold and silver thread. With no hesitation, the emperor's prefect, Asinius Pelagius, slid his sword from its sheath and bent the shaking slave over the oak table. He cleaved the man's head off, but it took two sword strokes to finish the job. The blood dripped onto the floor as the body spasmed across the food on the table.

Asinius Pelagius was a shell of what he once was. The years had not been kind to him, and his mahogany skin was weathered like an ancient boot and twice as dry. He had gotten to a place where he was tired of complaining of how old war wounds plagued him on the coldest and rainiest days. The physicians told him he needed more exercise, but the last time he ran or rode a horse was during the campaign to crush the Ba warriors twenty-five years before. They were a class of warriors who sold humans as a means of survival living in the Lava Lands.

Few, if any, legionnaires like him survived the Battle of the Lava Lands. The Wolfryian losses were catastrophic. Emperor Tiberius, Octavius's father, lost three-quarters of his men, over two thousand hardened soldiers. And the ones like Asinius did not have fond memories of the battle . . . only the carnage.

He had the look of an old, grizzled veteran. His red eye patch covering his right eye was tight against his gaunt face. He tried to keep his salt-and-pepper beard trimmed daily, but his hands usually shook in the morning. He wasn't sure, but he was forgetting random things throughout the day as well. His beard was a style from days past when prefects were worth something, but their respect had died amongst the peasants and the aristocracy when Tiberius was murdered. Asinius took a haggard breath and thought of the battle that changed world history. Like a bolt of thunder, a thought came to him.

"Front rank, kneel," Asinius shouted.

The veterans took the command in stride, the legionnaires familiar with the sound of his voice. They stood shoulder to shoulder.

"Who are the better legionnaires today?" he roared, slamming his visor down behind them.

"Legion 1, m'lord," they responded with a cheer before kneeling like a well-oiled machine.

Across the landscape, the Ba warriors rode across the plain, their mounts leaping across the dead pooled in the middle of the battlefield. With a loud roar, the lion men crashed into the front line of Legion 1, slaughtering most of the first rank. Asinius heard their screams and the roar of the warriors as he battled for his life. His horse was cut down, and he tumbled from the saddle. One of his men helped him to his feet as a lance burst through his back. The blood splattered across Asinius's face as another legionnaire impaled the warrior.

Asinius wiped his face across his sleeve, then attacked, slashed, and hacked limbs from their massive eight-foot frames, ducking, spinning, and slaughtering. Four fell at his feet before the second regiment behind sprinted into the mix.

A loud horn sounded on his left, then on his right as the warriors retreated. As they drew back for another charge, Asinius's men hurried to reform. Tiberius rode forward to Asinius's position to see the battle up close, his retainers floating in front of him, shields held high for any stray arrows.

"End this, now," Tiberius shouted, sitting in the saddle next to Asinius.

Asinius swung his blood- and fur-covered blade in front of his face and then raised his sword above his head. "On me, you bastards," he commanded, remounting a fresh horse.

His men stood up and marched forward to space themselves from the dead. Out of the corner of his eye, Asinius watched several Ba warriors galloping into their flank, buying time for their shield brothers to regroup.

Asinius watched as the riders bore down on Tiberius. He pointed his sword at the emperor behind him.

"To the Emperor!"

Asinius slammed his heels into his horse's flanks and rode back to the emperor, followed by twelve of his hardened centurions in red-plumed helmets. He dismounted in front of Tiberius's horse. A broken pike lay in front of him. He snatched it and posted it against the inside of his boot just as the riders slammed into them, their lances aimed low.

Asinius heard the roars a few feet away. Before he could blink, the warriors crashed into him and his men. Asinius thrust his pike up and gored the lead rider in the chest. Another rider on his right with a red rope tied around the tip of his lance aimed it at him. Asinius's mind raced, then slowed to a crawl as the spearhead floated into his view.

The lance penetrated Asinius's armor and slammed into his hip. Before the warrior could slam his spear through him, one of his centurions launched a pilum into the air, tumbling the warrior from the saddle.

Asinius ground his teeth and gave a deep growl, then fell into one of his men. He spat the phlegm from his parched throat, then freed his sword. He yanked the broken lance from his hip and screamed in pain. Another warrior closed in, and three of his centurions stepped in front of him and engaged. The few warriors fell quickly, then Asinius collapsed. He stayed conscious long enough to see his fellow leaders, Peltasius and Maria Atticus, lead his men forward to slaughter the remaining warriors. Then he passed out.

He woke up several hours later in a medical tent with Tiberius hovering over him.

"You're still alive?" Tiberius asked.

Asinius nodded and stared at his shattered hip.

"I am promoting you to prefect for your sacrifice. You saved my life, and for that, I am grateful. Heal up and then report to the castle for your new assignment," Tiberius said.

Asinius could only nod, the pain too great for him to speak. The emperor withdrew with his entourage and left Asinius to revel in his glory.

Asinius snapped back to reality and glared at the slaves cowering in the corner. He touched his hip and winced, even though the pain was long gone. He motioned for the others to pull the headless body from the table. He picked up the slave's severed head and threw it to the dogs below. Octavius roared with laughter, slapping his thigh as he watched the hounds tear the head to pieces, then each other.

"Asinius, you always know my wishes before they reach my mind," he said, picking up a handful of ripe purple grapes from the table.

Octavius shoved them in his mouth with a grunt and then grabbed a leg of mutton. With a satisfying groan and an eye roll, he was in bliss. Food was one of the boy-king's greatest pleasures, other than his sexual debauchery.

The throne he sat on was made from the bones of Rebellium commanders neatly stacked on top of one another. They sat on top of a base made of solid gold, surrounded by skulls that had been dipped in liquid silver.

Wolfryians believed to sit on your dead enemies was a sign of the gods favoring them. His father's throne had been made of stone, but blood stained it. It was a constant reminder for those who failed to protect him.

Octavius had it broken into smaller pieces and placed around the dais below him as a reminder of what happened when his father let his guard down. He firmly believed compassion for the masses killed his father, and he wouldn't make the same mistake.

"More wine," he shouted. Another slave approached and stood in a pool of blood, hands trembling. The man tried to concentrate on not dropping the lead-lined carafe as his pulse quickened. Octavius stared at the slave as he bent over to retrieve the dirty bowls. The man managed to marshal the goblets and silverware onto a tray without passing out.

Octavius stared at his rear end. He licked his lips as the man's toga slipped up to his midthigh. When the slave finished, Octavius motioned for him to lean forward. "Come to my room later with a few of the others, and I will show you the meaning of lust," he said.

He ran his stubby pinky finger with a long, yellow fingernail along the slave's ear, cooing sweet nothings into it. The slave blushed, bowed his head, and then left. Octavius licked his lips again and stared at him as he walked away.

He gave Asinius a wink and muttered, "I love slave cock. Don't you, Prefect?"

"They are not my first choice, Imperator." He shook his head in disgust as he watched the emperor fart and then burp as he reached for more food.

Octavius's favorite food was mutton and pork, but he recently started having headaches at the back of his head and neck, so he tried to cut back . . . a feat too difficult to master. His eyes turned cold.

"Asinius, why have we not found that traitor, Viridius?"

"Viridius will continue to escape us if we keep sending mercenaries after him, Imperator," Asinius said.

"Then who shall we send?" Octavius asked.

Asinius shrugged. "We may need help from the Answari, or we will continue to have body parts sent back to us. I don't know who can kill him," Asinius said.

"What about you?" Octavius asked, raising an eyebrow.

"Imperator, I'm an old legionnaire who wouldn't stand a chance against him. We fought together, and I saw him kill more men than I could count. If I go, I'm a dead man," Asinius said.

Octavius stopped eating and wiped the back of his hand over his lips. A quizzical look crossed his features as he smacked his lips together. "What good are you as my prefect then, Asinius?" He held his hand to his temple and rubbed it. "My head is pounding again. Fetch me some of my belladonna flowers."

Octavius was not in good health, his stature far from impressive. He was short, barely taller than a boy of twelve. And when he drank, he usually tortured and maimed people with a wave of his hand. He was indifferent when it came to torture, especially women and children. They meant nothing to him.

After his father was assassinated, Octavius became indifferent to death. A piece of him died with his father, and then he withdrew with his belladonna leaves and became distant to everyone, even his closest advisors.

Asinius believed that's where the change had occurred, like most others in the court. Octavius was always a mysterious child, prone to pranks and bouts of laughter, but where a child was, a drugged tyrannical half-wit stood in his place.

The belladonna leaves helped influence his decision to kill the empress of Wolfryia and then cut her into a thousand pieces. He had her ground up and fed to the poor because she didn't tickle his fancy any longer.

Deep in thought, Octavius moved his index finger under his nostrils as droplets of blood fell onto his toga. He glanced around, saw no one was watching, and then spilled wine over the center of his toga to cover the stains.

"I need a new toga," he roared.

His slaves rushed from the room and brought a freshly pressed replacement. They helped him undress, his bloated figure in clear view of Asinius, who turned his head in disgust.

Usually, Octavius's nose bled daily, but he had been - able to cover it up for the most part. It seemed the more he drank and chewed belladonna leaves, the worse it became.

A sharp knock sounded behind the four-inch-thick oak doors at the front of the throne room. They creaked open, the hinges in need of oil. A group of men walked in. The palace guards snapped to attention as the group walked by, their boots clicking on the black marble.

Asinius raised his hand in the air with a closed fist, signaling his men to stand at the ready. Three guards broke formation and stood in front of the dais steps with their spears crossed.

The guards confiscated the men's weapons as they approached. Octavius was leery of anyone who approached him, and if he did meet with someone, even if they were his most trusted allies, they would be unarmed. The men who marched in were covered in mud and filth from the road. They knelt before the stairs as they approached, their red cloaks shred at the bottom.

The scale segmentata armor under their torn white tabards was bloodied from whatever fighting had recently taken place. The men placed their hands over their hearts.

"We are but dust in the wind, Imperator," they said in unison.

The recent skirmish they were in was at the edge of the Batopian wilderness when they went in search of Viridius for the tenth time. No Wolfryians were welcome over the border, and if they did cross over, their tabards were returned torched from the fire where they were burned at the stake.

Not saying anything in response, Octavius nodded and held his hand out. A large ruby in a platinum setting hung from his left pinky. The leader of the small band approached the steps with his standard-bearer and attempted to ascend them. As they neared Asinius, the standard-bearer slammed his lance onto the marble.

"Imperator, Lord
    has returned."

The Wolfryian flag that hung by the standard-bearer's side was white with a bust of Octavius's face at the center, and this one was splashed with blood. Before taking his first step, Asinius held a vine branch across the man's chest.

"Watch yourself, Marus."

"Touch me again, Cripple, and I'll gut you. Now, move," Marus said, pushing past him.

Asinius smiled and stepped aside. Marus reached the top step quickly and approached the throne. He put his hand under Octavius's, held it, and took a knee. "We have returned, Imperator."

"Lord Marus Atticus, commander of Legion I. What news of your mission?" Octavius asked, looking for his belladonna leaves.

Asinius walked over and handed them to him. Not turning his head, Octavius shoved the leaves in his mouth and stuck them in his bottom gum line.

"Imperator, we were ambushed, and I lost most of my men. I believe Viridius is in the fishing village of Pistoryum on the northern coast, but we couldn't get there," Marus reported.

"I don't care where he is, and I care not that you were ambushed! I want him dead, stuffed, and in my hall by the summer. Do you understand me?" he screeched.

"I need only hear to obey, Imperator," Marus replied, bowing lower.

Octavius inhaled deeply. "I don't need your poetry, Marus. I need your skill in tracking my prey. Hell, it should be easy. Haven't I killed everything he ever loved?"

"You have, Imperator, right down to his dogs," Marus said.

"Then bring me his head," Octavius hissed.

Marus nodded and bowed again before standing up.

"You may stand next to Asinius," Octavius said with a wave of his hand.

Marus walked over and stood near Asinius, trying his best not to hiss an insult at his bitter rival. Marus's heart was cold, twisted . . . sinister, even. Old Answari heritage showed in his easy tan and jet-black hair recently began to thin, and streaks of silver had started to run through it. He carried the title of Legatus, which he was proud to carry.

A Wolfryian legatus was Octavius's mouthpiece. They were his private police force sent to find any disloyal politicians and legionnaires. He was a wolf in sheep's clothing and tried to keep the emperor's ear at all times. He knew if he lost it, it would mean a loss of favor and the unlimited power that came with it. And he would end up like Asinius, which he dreaded.

Octavius processed what he was being told and then pushed himself off the throne and stumbled toward Marus, hallucinating. Octavius slapped him across the face with the back of his hand, the spit from the corner of his mouth peppering Marus's armor. More annoyed than hurt, Marus instinctively reached for the knife at his side.

The guards could hear Marus suck in a deep breath as he remembered it had been confiscated. Before he could move his hand from his waist, a knife was at his throat from behind. Asinius pressed it against his jugular, then yanked his head back. Marus swallowed the lump in his throat, his palms sweaty.

"Your orders, Imperator?" Asinius asked, tightening his grip on Marus's hair.

"Orders, yes, kill . . . wait . . . where . . . Where am I? Asinius, why do *you* have a knife to my loyal commander Marus's throat? Marus, what the hell are you doing here? Where . . . Where the hell is that traitor, Viridius?" Octavius asked, rubbing his temples in confusion before he collapsed back onto the throne.

"Shit, here we go again," Asinius grumbled. "Guard, pick the emperor up and bring him to his chambers. You know the drill; two men at each window, four to the door. Move out."

One of the men picked up the emperor and cradled him in his arms as he threw up. The guard dropped him on his face and held his hands up in disgust with vomit smeared across his breastplate. The others put their hands over their mouths and tried to refrain from laughing.

Asinius stared down at the emperor and motioned his men to pick him up again. The guards carried him away to sleep it off, and Asinius secretly hoped he wouldn't wake up.

"I'll kill you for that, Asinius," Marus hissed before he descended the stairs to rejoin his men.

"Get in line," Asinius muttered before he walked out onto the balcony.

CHAPTER

Viridius

Tiberius's Assassination

Viridius strolled through the garden, his hand brushing against the thornbushes that pricked his palm. He smiled a sad smile. He knew the war with the Ba pridesmen would end soon, and it would most likely be his death in the final, unsinkable battle.

He snapped a violet flower off its stem and turned to his wife, Alecta. Brushing her copper-toned hair off her ear, he slid the flower behind it. She smiled and brushed her hand against his.

"I love you," she whispered.

"As do I," he said, staring into her eyes.

His father had arranged their courtship, and it combined the two most powerful houses among the lesser lords of

Wolfryia, some no more than brigands, like Viridius's lineage line.

"I have to go to the palace and tend to Emperor Tiberius," he said as they approached the villa.

Their villa was a gift from the emperor. Viridius was still shocked by the gift, a rare glimpse of goodness from an otherwise deranged man. He marveled at the bleached, white-speckled stucco glistening in the early-morning mist and the trees he had planted with Alecta that adorned the front yard.

"I love the oak trees we planted," he said, gazing up at the leafy limbs.

"Me too," she said.

He sighed and winked at her. "Gotta be going. I'll see you later in the throne room," he said, pecking her on the cheek.

"You certainly will," she said with a sly smile.

He watched her enter the villa and then mounted his horse. He cantered out of the courtyard and passed the peasants leading their carts to the trade district.

What a beautiful day, he thought as he rode under the portcullis.

He saluted the guards in the watchtower and continued down the road. His horse trotted to the stable where he dismounted. A stable boy ran up and took the reins from him.

Viridius smiled and flipped him a gold coin. "Don't spend it all in one place," he said with a grin.

He strode the short distance to the palace, saluted the guards, and walked into the throne room. Tiberius sat on the throne listening to Viridius's father, Rotix, and his brother, Palix. They were talking about something, but he couldn't hear from where he was standing. He was the junior officer and unable to attend the meeting with senior prefects, even though they were family. Court rules were court rules, after all.

Tiberius waved him toward the steps. Viridius bowed and held his blue stole from falling onto the ground.

"Imperator," he said, approaching the throne.

"Viridius, prepare the throne room for the poor to collect their stipends," Tiberius muttered, rubbing his temples with a sigh.

Viridius bowed again and made eye contact with his father and brother. They only made eye contact for a moment and then went back to talking to the emperor. As they spoke, the poor were led in by the Imperial Guard.

Viridius's father and brother stood behind Tiberius, their eyes searching the crowd for any perceived threat.

A herald stood atop the stairs and shouted, "Our exalted emperor Tiberius Victorus will now give out your monthly stipends."

The guards shoved the peasants into line as they fought each other to be first in line. Viridius glanced at his father and brother, who stood side by side behind the emperor, whispering to each other. Their eyes darted around the room, surveying for any threats.

It all happened so fast that had Viridius blinked he would have missed it. Then it was over. A loud distraction at the side door beside the throne for the emperor to enter and exit drew everyone's attention from the emperor.

Several men broke through the mass of people, hacking and slashing at the guards lined up with their backs to the door.

Viridius drew his sword and shouted, "Protect the emperor!"

A woman standing next to Viridius screamed as a man knocked him to the ground. Viridius looked up and saw blood running down the steps. Several of the Imperial Guardsmen lay with their throats cut, their swords still in their scabbards.

A quizzical look crossed Viridius's face as he watched his father and brother pull their knives from Tiberius's back and hurtle him down the steps. Viridius didn't have time to think. The man who knocked him down swung his sword at him.

Viridius knocked the blade to the side, cut the man's shins with his own blade, and then kicked him away. He regained his feet, shoved his sword through the man attacking him, and then sprinted for the throne. His brother and father pulled their swords and crossed them in front of their faces.

"Move aside, son. This was bound to happen," his father said.

Viridius extended his arm and expelled a thin blade with no handle. It hit his brother in the throat. Palix fell to his knees, eyes wide. As his body rolled down the stone steps toward the emperor, Viridius engaged his father.

"I'll kill you," Viridius roared. "You killed the emperor!"

His father took a step back and freed his second blade. "It had to be done, son. No one man should have all the power."

The two battled for several moments, attempting to find weaknesses. As Viridius forced Rotix back, Rotix slipped on some blood. Viridius seized the moment and ran him through. His father's warm blood flooded over his bare hands, staining them.

Rotix glanced up with a smile, blood dripping from his lips. "For the Rebe—"

Viridius thrust his wrist dagger under Rotix's chin, cutting his sentence short. He kicked his father off the blade and down the steps. He exhaled loudly and then rushed to the emperor and knelt by his side. Gripping Tiberius's trembling hand, Viridius moved his head into his lap.

"I failed you, Imperator," Viridius whispered.

Tiberius's lips twitched, and his eyes went wide as a low sigh escaped his lips. Asinius rushed in with his guardsmen holding Viridius's wife and best friend, Gius Flavius. Asinius stared at the body of the emperor and shouted, "Arrest the assassin!"

Viridius stood up and said, "I killed the men responsible," he said, pointing to the bodies of Rotix and Palix.

Asinius gave him a cold stare and pushed his wife to the ground. "*You're* the assassin." He gestures to the guardsmen. "Now, arrest this traitor."

Octavius stormed into the room, spittle dripping from his lips. He saw his father at the foot of the steps and ran to him. Sobs wracked his body as he cradled his father's head.

Viridius heard him muttering, "No, no, it can't be. Someone help him!"

Asinius walked over to Octavius and put his hand on his shoulder. He whispered into his ear and then stood beside him.

A guardsman slammed Viridius over a mahogany table from behind and tied his hands behind his back. He stood him up as Octavius walked over, tears falling from his eyes. He slapped Viridius across the face, stood nose to nose to him, and hissed, "You'll pay for this." He stormed past Asinius and walked out of the throne room with his guards in tow.

A guardsman shoved Viridius toward the door. "Move!"

Viridius reached out to his wife. "Alecta, Alecta, what is happening?"

She cast her eyes to the floor. "It had to be done."

Viridius recoiled from the verbal blow and glared at Gius as he walked by.

"Sorry about this. Never expected you to survive," Gius said with a shrug of his shoulder. "Dumb luck, I guess."

Viridius paled and then slammed his forehead against Gius's nose and sent him crashing to the floor. The guards stuck their swords to Viridius's throat.

Asinius held his hands up. "No. We will torture him for information to see who else in the city was involved. Bring him to the cells."

The guards marched Viridius to a holding cell deep within the bowels of the castle. They unbound his wrists and shoved him in, then slammed the door shut.

"Rot in hell, traitor," one of the men said, spitting on him.

Numb to emotion, Viridius allowed the spit to drip from his chin. *I can't believe this is happening.*

His eyes searched the cold, bare room. There were no windows, only a bucket to shit in. The hay had been recently removed, and he had a suspicion they wouldn't be bringing it back.

He sat down on the ice-cold ground, his back against the slimy wall. He stared at his hands, the blood drying on his fingertips. The smell made him vomit. He spat into his palms, trying to rub it off with his blue stole, but to no avail. He stared at his coveted stole in disgust and threw it to the other side of the room. His whole life had changed in the blink of an eye.

I killed my father and brother. Forgive me, Gods.

For the first time in his adult life, he cried, not because of what he did, but because he knew they would sentence Alecta to death because of his failure. He dried his eyes and looked around, ensuring sure no one saw him.

The guard sat on a stool, kicked his feet up, and leaned his head back. "Traitor, I need some rest before we torture you. I was out all night with my girl."

He picked up a pebble near his foot and threw it against the opposite wall. It made a clinking sound and then rolled away.

The guard raised his chin. He slapped his spear butt against the iron bars. "Quiet," he mumbled before dozing back off.

Viridius stood up and paced the cell. He soon found what he was searching for. A sharp piece of stone stuck out from the wall by his foot. He coughed loudly to conceal any noise and broke it off with a quick stomp.

He heard a voice down the hall yell, "Brutus, prepare the prefect. We will come and get him in an hour."

Viridius knew precisely what that meant. Getting information was what this guard did best. He was one of the best torturers with hot iron pliers in the castle. People would say anything to make him stop. Viridius picked up the rock and felt along the edges. Jagged and formidable, it was a simple, brutish, killing machine. He looked around the room and knew what to do. He slammed his palms against the wall and gasped for breath. As he clutched his chest, he fell to one knee. "Please, help," he mumbled, pulling on his neckline.

The guard glanced over his shoulder with a sigh, stood up, and flung the door open. "What's the matter? You having a heart attack?" he asked.

As the guard lowered his head to check on him, Viridius slammed his makeshift knife under his chin. The blow didn't kill him instantly. He lingered for a few moments clutching at Viridius's tunic, his blood gushing from the wound.

Without much effort, Viridius pushed the rock up further and finished him. Quickly, he lowered the man to the floor, then stripped him. The pants were too tight, and the shirt made him look like he had one too many dinners. But the shoes . . . The shoes fit well.

He pulled the guard's hauberk on and adjusted his helmet. The spear lay by the cell door, and he quickly picked it up. He broke the shaft over his knee as another guard walked down the steps. Viridius sat where the guard had been sitting and lowered his head onto his chest. The other guard walked up and nudged Viridius with his boot.

"Brutus, I'm not covering for you if you're drunk again, you ass. Get up," he hissed, jabbing his spear into Viridius's ribs.

Viridius glanced up. "Surprise," he said, jamming the broken spearhead into the man's groin.

The guard flopped to the ground, blood dripping from the corners of his mouth. Viridius got to his feet, dragged the guard inside the cell, and then ran for the stairwell.

He navigated his way through the dungeon, stopping only to drink from the pools of stagnant water puddling in the crevices of the wall.

Finally, after what seemed like a hallway that would never end, he reached the main floor of the castle. As he exited, he saw Alecta's mangled corpse hanging from the tower, her tongue protruding from between her blue lips.

The other members of the Rebellium swung next to her from thick strands of rope. He took a step toward her body, but a group of legionnaires ran past him. He ducked back into the shadows of the buildings.

I'm sorry, Alecta.

A single tear fell from the corner of his eye. He searched the area and saw a horse tethered to a rail near him. He untied it, slipped into the saddle, and rode off toward the Batopian wilderness.

CHAPTER

Four

Where the hell am I? Viridius asked himself, searching the room.

He searched for anything that might cause him harm, and with a pained grunt, he pushed himself up to his knees. He noticed Gius asleep in a chair, his chin resting on his chest.

Gius was a few years older than Viridius. His crooked teeth were stained brown from the tobacco he chewed. His curly black hair had one silver streak running through it, making him look more like a skunk than a legionnaire.

With his eyes closed, Gius said, "Morning."

Viridius attempted to shake the cobwebs from his hungover brain. *How did he find me?* he thought.

Viridius rose to his feet and coughed. Gius lowered the legs of the chair back to the floor that he was sleeping in and stood up with a full stretch, then took a step forward.

"Are you open to hearing my plan yet, Viridius?"

"What plan?" he asked, trying to recall how he got here.

"Killing the emperor," Gius said.

A lightbulb went off, and he nodded, running his hand over his bruised skull. "All right, I'm listening."

A slick smile crossed Gius's lips.

Nonchalantly, Viridius asked, "What do you need me for, Gius? I'm not your answer." He glanced down and said, "I kill without remorse. Some find this valuable, and others find it disturbing. Is that the skill you seek?" he asked, feeling his tunic.

Gius pointed to a dry tunic hanging by the hearth. "That's *precisely* what I need."

Viridius nodded his thanks and pulled his tunic over his head. He flung it over his shoulder and then grabbed the one drying nearby.

Gius went to his satchel near the door and pulled out a stained and bloody piece of parchment. After unrolling it, he read it to Viridius.

I, Octavius Victorus, hereby authorize the extermination of any and all members of the Rebellium, men and women found guilty in absentia for the murder of my father, Emperor Tiberius Victorus. These citizens must be brought to justice and punished for their disloyalty. The person at the top of this list must be crucified for his crime and burned at the stake. Bring me Viridius Vispanius. Find him, torture him, and kill his family and friends. But his heart and head belong to me.

Emperor Octavius of Wolfryia

Gius rolled it up and eyed him. "Found this on a man I killed a few months ago. You do know you still have a price on your head?" Gius asked.

"I know," he said, a slight smile at the corner of his lips. "Killed everyone they've sent."

Viridius wanted to be left alone, and it looked like that idea was slowly being snuffed out. Pausing, he sighed and put his fingers on his chin. *Well, looks like all I am is a killer. Once a killer, always a killer.*

Interrupting his thoughts, Gius said, "I know you want revenge, but you can't do it from here. They will just keep coming for you and staying here puts all these peasants in danger. Ride with me, and we can rid the world of tyrants."

Ignoring Gius, Viridius walked over to the water basin and washed his face free of the vomit and debris. After a few moments of silence, Viridius chuckled and dried his face on a nearby linen cloth.

"Tell me why I should give a damn if these peasants die. They ain't my people." Their eyes met, and Viridius's tone became icy. "I've lost the person who mattered the most. You should remember that. So, no, I won't help you. I'll get my revenge on *my* terms, *not* on yours."

Gius shook his head and sighed. "I must have the wrong man. The Viridius I knew was no coward. Good day to you," he said curtly, opening the door, his hand slowly moving toward the blade stuffed in the back of his breeches.

"That's more like it. Now back to the tavern I go. Good luck in your quest to save Dellos, Gius. I'll be right at home with the whores and fatherless children waiting for my moment." He spat at Gius's feet and glanced up. "I ain't the man you came to find. I'm just a washed-up prefect," he whispered, patting Gius on the shoulder.

Gius sighed and pulled his hand from the knife handle. He would kill Viridius when he was asleep just to put him out of his misery. No use draining his life force out as he stared into Viridius's pathetic eyes. Gius watched his former best friend amble toward the stairs. Viridius's feet crossed midstep, and he tumbled down the rest of them like a tumbleweed.

"Poor bastard," Gius muttered, closing the door.

The patrons didn't even glance at the bleeding lump of flesh at the foot of the stairs. With only his pride damaged, Viridius crawled to the banister and pulled himself up. Once he regained his legs, he brushed himself off and walked to the tavern door, head held high. As he reached it, the door swung inward and knocked him to the floor.

Three rugged mercenaries strolled in and glanced at the patrons' faces. They wore white tabards that were freshly pressed with a black ax and a red spear crossed on the front, the sign of Wolfryian bounty hunters. Viridius took one look at the men and knew who they were.

Can't these bastards leave me be?

The leader of the group walked to the innkeeper and glared at him. "I'm looking Viridius Vispanius. Seen him?"

For a brief moment, the innkeeper paused, not sure what to say. He shook his head no. "I haven't m—"

The leader of the group snatched the innkeeper's shoulder and stabbed him in the neck. The patrons stared at the blood dripping from the mahogany ledge as the man's body collapsed.

The leader turned around and said, "Now that I have everyone's attention, who knows the whereabouts of the former prefect, Viridius Vispanius?"

No one spoke, nor did they move. They were there to get drunk and forget their past—not to memorize who came and went in their seedy inn. "Oh, did no one hear me?" he asked, looking around.

A wicked smile crossed his features when he noticed Viridius on the ground, who did the best he could to hide, but even with his body in a halfhearted dead pose, they knew. Mercs always know what they hunt: flesh or money.

"Looky who we have here, boys," the man said, glancing at his companions. "On your feet, you worthless piece of shit. Been hunting you for a while. It's about time I found you."

A crossbow bolt grazed the leader's ear and sank into one of the attacker's chests behind him. The man glanced at the bolt and then fell to his knees. The mercenary's sword dropped from his hand and clattered on the floor near Viridius.

Someone jerked Viridius up and held him in a choke hold as a human shield. He squirmed, trying to free himself as another bolt hit the second attacker who was charging the stairwell.

The man bounded up five steps and then came rolling back down. A bolt stuck out of his forehead, and as he hit the floor, the shaft broke off. Blood flowed out in front of the stairs as Gius descended from above with a limp. The soles of his boots were soaked with blood as he reached the bottom floor.

"I would let him go if I were you," Gius said, reloading his crossbow, his voice like steel. He crossed into the light and pointed his handheld crossbow at his target.

"Gius Flavius, I thought you might be floating 'round here. I always knew you were alive. Guess I should have checked under your hood when you were brought to the gallows. A mistake I won't make twice," the man said, trying to hide behind Viridius.

"Last warning, Viscus," Gius said, circling him.

Viridius growled. "Viscus . . ."

Gius circled Viscus and stopped. "Last chance."

"You wouldn't da—"

Gius pulled the knife from his waistband and threw it at Viscus before he could react. The weapon went end over end and embedded in his skull. Blood smeared across Viridius's cheek as the body fell backward.

"Been waiting a long time for that moment," Gius muttered, pulling his blade free. "He was partly responsible for killing my kids," he said as he turned around, his face flushed.

Viridius felt compassion for his old friend for a moment and then chuckled as he knelt next to Viscus. He bit into a gold coin he found in Viscus's pocket.

"This is real gold. And I bet he has more." He ripped Viscus's tabard open, and with a laugh, he cut a coin pouch hanging around his neck. "Yup, I was right."

He shook the pouch near his ear and heard the clinking coins inside. "Oh, a private stash. These coins are what I'm looking for," he said, flipping one in Gius's direction. "Go find a whore."

Gius rested his blade over Viridius's shoulder and lifted his head. "I disapprove of your looting habits. The dead are not to be picked clean. It angers the gods," Gius hissed.

Viridius pushed the blade away, muttered under his breath, and continued his looting. "He has gold teeth. I always knew Viscus was an idiot," Viridius said.

"Have you no decency?" Gius demanded.

Viridius yanked the teeth from Viscus's mouth, stood up, and then urinated on his corpse. With a sinister smile, he said, "Decency . . . nope, fresh out. He's lucky you killed him. I wish I could bring him back to life and kill him again."

"Ugh."

"We best be going," Viridius said.

"So, you're in?" Gius asked, regaining his composure.

Viridius felt the blood on his neck. "Ain't got a choice now. Can't hide here anymore."

He zipped his pants up with a grunt and then sprinted outside. Gius followed behind him and jumped on his horse. He pointed at the mule tethered next to Viridius.

Glancing down at him with a smug smile, Gius said, "It's the only animal I could find for sale in this shithole. And I paid a fortune for it. Worthless thing cost me a thousand Wolfryian coins. So, hurry up and get on."

The mule swung its tail and hit Viridius in the face with a loud bray. Viridius slapped the mule on the ass and said, "Gius, I ain't riding this thing. I'd rather walk."

"Suit yourself. I'm riding out," Gius said, holding his hand over his brow. "Look, over the horizon," he stated, pointing his finger at the dust cloud beyond the ridge.

Viridius watched the dust for a moment. "You know, on second thought," he glanced at Gius and then the dust cloud as it moved closer, "I'm going to ride with you after all."

"There's probably too many to fight. We'll have to hide. We'll lose them in the forest," Gius said.

Awkwardly, Viridius mounted the mule painted like a zebra.

Who the fuck would paint a mule?

Shouting over his shoulder, Gius said, "Keep up or die. Same rules apply like they did in our old unit."

After riding through the night and taking multiple shortcuts through the Whispering Woods, they managed to lose the bounty hunters.

The Whispering Woods was where the Batopian wilderness began. It was said to be haunted by the souls of fallen legionnaires who deserted and were killed by their own men. Viridius and Gius took a break halfway through the forest to let the animals rest near a secluded pond. Gius went on foot in search of food, and Viridius started a small fire.

An hour later, Gius came back with several rabbits hanging from a tree branch. Neither man talked while Gius prepared dinner. Viridius puffed on his pipe and blew smoke rings into the air as he leaned his sore back against a tree.

He finally broke the silence and said, "They say this woodland has demons, killer trees, and other creatures just as terrible in the vast darkness." He glanced around after he said it, staring at every tree to make sure they didn't move.

Gius laughed and pointed to a tree with a wind chime hanging from it, hidden to anyone who didn't know it was there. "There are your ghosts. A tribe of wild men who don't live far from here uses it as a scare tactic. They have helped the Rebellium from time to time," he said, turning the rabbit over he had on the skewer.

"Can they help us reach your fort?" Viridius asked.

"Doubtful. They only protect themselves. There are only a handful of warriors with no wives. They worship the god Eltel," he replied.

"The God of Death?" Viridius asked, pausing between puffs.

"Yes, the very same. The men who wander in here in search of treasure usually become their sacrifices. The Rebellium brings the tribesmen food for free passage through their land. The others . . ." he snapped his fingers, "shouldn't tread here." Gius laughed and continued, "The surprise is there is no treasure."

Viridius pushed himself to his feet with a smile, walked over to where Gius was sitting, and said, "Must have gone pretty bad for you to come out of hiding, old man. Pistoryum is a dangerous place for someone like you."

"Someone like me?"

"Yea, you know. A big, wet, pus—"

Before he could finish his statement, Gius elbowed him in the balls. He fell to his knees and held his crotch, gasping for air.

"You dirty rott—" Viridius muttered through clenched teeth.

Gius snatched Viridius's tunic, closed his fist, and then punched him across the jaw. Knocked unconscious, Viridius crumpled at his feet.

"A wet pussy." Gius snorted. "I'll give you a wet pussy."

He picked Viridius's pipe up, rubbed the stem on his tunic, and then gingerly lit it. Gius dragged his friend under a tree by his feet, smiling every time he heard his head bounce over a rock in their path. After securing him to the tree, Gius returned to the fire and continued preparing his meal.

CHAPTER

Octavius's snores woke up the male slave in his bed. One slave slipped out from under his flabby arm and woke him up. Octavius yawned and looked around the room as the sunrise illuminated it.

He struggled for a few minutes to get out of bed. Finally, a slave helped him up, then lay down beside the bed. The slave wore a soft brown bearskin so that the emperor's naked feet never felt the cold marble. The man grimaced in pain as Octavius stood on his back and stretched.

Every morning, the emperor stepped on a different slave to remind them of who was in charge. The bedchamber was lavish, his bathtub was made of gelded gold, and his goblets and silverware were made by the best silver and lead smiths in Dellos.

All of his togas were made from the finest imported silk, courtesy of the Answari. His balcony overlooked the city of Iceport in its entirety. The city was named Iceport because of the large blue and red icebergs floating in the bay's semifrozen ocean.

His slaves threw rose petals out in front of him as he walked over to a bubbling hot tub. He dipped his toe in to test the water and moaned. "Ahhhh."

He lowered his naked body into the water and sighed. The slaves washed him above the water and below as he lay his head onto the tub's edge.

He made eye contact with a younger slave and nodded at his crotch. The slave removed his own toga and washed Octavius's penis under the water.

One of the slaves handed Octavius a cup of wine. After taking a few gulps, the slave took the goblet back and gently wiped his mouth. Octavius licked his lips and stared at the man. The man shaved Octavius's face and massaged his shoulders. He did his best to ignore the emperor's gaze, but he felt his eyes undressing him.

A polite knock sounded from outside the bedchamber. One of the guards looked at the emperor, who waved his hand dismissively. The guard opened the door, and two guards crossed their spears in front of the emperor. The men who entered stood and waited for the spearmen to move.

"Let them pass," Octavius said, glancing around one of the guards. The spears lifted, and Asinius approached the tub.

"Imperator, what are your wishes?" Asinius asked.

Octavius closed his eyes and leaned back again, letting his naked slave work his hand below the water. He groaned in pleasure as he lifted his head.

"Asinius, why are you disturbing my morning rituals?" Octavius managed to gasp.

"Imperator, Marus came to report his findings this morning," Asinius said.

"And?" Octavius asked.

"He's outside. I haven't heard his report because you slapped him across the face for his failure to find Viridius, and then he attacked you last night. Do you not remember, Imperator?" Asinius asked.

"It's a little hazy for me at the moment," he said, raising his head from the ledge of the tub. "Did you say he attacked me, Prefect?"

"Ye—"

Octavius waved his hand to stop him from answering and said, "I must have started it. Marus is more loyal than you could ever hope to be, Asinius. I don't know why I bother keeping you around. You're just a lazy, worthless, crippled old goat. Now that you've ruined my morning ritual, I'll start my day."

Asinius's face darkened. He bristled at the insult but remained levelheaded. He clenched his right fist repeatedly until his knuckles popped.. After regaining his composure, he glared at Octavius's favored guards standing in front of him with arrogant smiles on their faces. He mouthed, *Fuck you.*

Bloated, Octavius rose from his bathwater. Asinius gagged and turned his head as a slave hurried to dress him in a robe. After putting on the robe, Octavius walked to his balcony and spat over the side and hit a woman pulling a cart below him, then smiled. He shrugged and spat again as she continued to struggle down the road. Asinius walked up from behind and stood next to him.

"Prefect, bring Marus to my chambers. I would like to talk to him about a mission I want carried out," Octavius said without looking at him.

"As you wish, Imperator."

An hour later, Asinius and Marus walked into Octavius's chambers. The emperor was sitting at a table, eating a roasted turkey leg.

"More wine," he shouted, ringing a bell by his side.

Bowing at the waist as he got closer to the table, Marus said, "Imperator."

"Ah, Marus, my most trusted and loyal scout; come closer."

Marus gave a sly smile and a wink to Asinius, then stepped in front of him. Asinius clasped his hands behind his back, trying to refrain from striking him. A low growl escaped his lips as he watched Marus walk over to Octavius.

Octavius flicked his wrist as if he were an annoying fruit fly and said, "You are dismissed, worthless ape—I mean, Asinius."

The emperor's bootlick guards chuckled at his misfortune. Asinius paused and tried to control his temper. He took a step forward as he reached for a knife in a sheath attached to his forearm, then caught himself. Instead, he bowed low and touched his forehead. After the emperor was no longer looking at him, he left the room.

"Marus, I have an assignment for you," Octavius said, oblivious to the previous day's events.

"As you wish, Imperator. What do you ask of me?"

Glancing around, he waved Marus closer to him and whispered in his ear, his voice an octave higher.

"Your first order of business is to execute Asinius. You're my new prefect. He's trying to take my crown." Octavius's eyes flicked widely in their sockets. "He cannot be trusted," he hissed, spit leaking from the corner of his mouth. "He's an ape—a traitor to the crown."

Marus pulled his head back, noticing the dribble of spit from the corner of Octavius's mouth, and said, "Are you sure that's what you want, Imperator?"

Marus asked him quietly, so he had an option to turn back. The emperor killed on a whim. He had an air of indifference about crucifixions and beheadings. It was, after all, the best way to keep the populace loyal.

"Yes. Why would I say it if I didn't want it done?" Octavius spat, the white spit continuing to drip from the corner of his mouth.

"He has men who are loyal to him in the castle and other places in Iceport, Imperator. What—"

"Kill them too. I want them all dead!" he screeched at the top of his lungs.

Marus put his fist over his heart and bowed his head.

"On me!" he shouted to his men as he stormed out of the chamber.

Asinius inspected his sparsely decorated room as his slaves packed his belongings. He was in the process of donning his armor when one of his loyal slaves, Herius, told him of the conversation between Marus and the emperor.

Not wasting time, Asinius ordered his men to form in a square formation in the courtyard of his villa. He limped down the steps, and when he reached the bottom, his breathing became labored. He felt a pain radiating over his shoulder, down his arm and pulsating above his heart.

"M'lord, we have assembled the men and have readied your escape route," said one of his commanders.

He grunted at the man and stared at what would no longer be his home by nightfall. Of course, he had seen the writing on the wall when he left the palace. Herius's warning was just a confirmation. He knew they could only hold the emperor's troops off for so long. He planned to fight a leapfrog defense and escape into the marsh with as many of his men as possible.

Herius handed Asinius his helmet made of a copper and zinc compound, painted with white pigment. Attached to the helmet was a palladium mask with a large teardrop under one of the eyes.

It was the helmet of Wolfryian prefects, and they were handed down from father to son as the succession went on through time.

To be a prefect, a man had to be of pure blood, pure Wolfryian blood. The bloodline would have had to extend back to the beginning of the empire, hundreds of years before. Some were descended from the officers and decorated veterans who marched with the first emperor, others were descended from the ancient blood pact between the empire and the Gobo. To avoid war the elders of the Answari clans had promised to fight for them for the empire. The Gobo were the spear head of the Answari, sworn to defend the people and their way of life. It was tragic really, the Gobo and a few others held on the the old ways, but the Answari and their way of life was practically gone, they were Wolfryan now, or Trammonian. Honor bound to a lost cause, protecting something dead as the ancestors who made the pact. A pact forced by a greedy bunch of leeches who had grown fat on blood not their own. Fucking aristocrats.

"The enemy approaches," one of his sentries positioned in the guard tower above him shouted.

"How far away?" Asinius shouted back.

The guard turned back around and shouted in pain. He grabbed his stomach, fell backward, and smashed into the square. His body made a sickening crunch as it landed among Asinius's other troops.

"I guess they're within arrow range," Asinius muttered to no one in particular.

"Your orders, m'lord?" one of his commanders asked.

Asinius grunted and walked to the center of the courtyard, rubbing his shoulder. "Close the square."

His men stood far enough apart to fight effectively, but not so far apart that they couldn't protect one another.

Asinius's riveted segmentata armor glistened as the sun beat down on them. He hoisted his tabard above his head, displaying the Wolfryian coat of arms.

"We are no longer Wolfryians. We're outlaws and will be hunted to the far reaches of Dellos. If you want to leave, go."

No one moved.

"No prisoners, no mercy!" he bellowed as he threw the tabard onto the ground in front of him and spat on it. For good measure, he rubbed his heel over it, smearing it with dirt. His men cheered and formed a tighter defensive formation.

Sweat poured down Asinius's leathery face and over his eye patch. The first ranks of the enemy, ill equipped from the haste of Marus's marching order, appeared over the hill.

"Ready your bows!" shouted one of his commanders.

Asinius spat again and raised his arm high, then brought it down. The first flight of arrows jumped from his men's bowstrings and over the wall of his villa. His soldiers cheered as the enemy screamed out in pain. But their cheers were short-lived as the retaliatory arrows landed among his men.

"Give 'em another volley, boys," shouted a commander, standing beside him. "They don't stand a chance, Lord Asinius."

Asinius smiled. He knew it would only be a matter of time before the legion broke through the courtyard's wooden gate.

"Archers to the top wall," Asinius shouted, slamming his mask over his face.

The archers ran to the wall and fired another three more volleys. Before they could recover, another volley answered theirs, knocking a handful of men into the courtyard ten feet below.

Asinius looked for his archery commander after they blocked the next flight of arrows. The commander was sprawled out beside him, an arrow standing straight up in one of his eye sockets.

"Damn the Wolfryian aristocracy," Asinius mumbled, picking a wounded man up off the ground.

He sent him back to the rear where a healer was treating the wounded. Another volley came in as Asinius's back was turned. One of his men shielded him as the arrows rained down. Asinius pushed himself up, but the man's weight on his back was too much for him to move.

"Get off me, soldier," Asinius shouted, his helmet a few yards away.

The weight on his back eased, and Herius pulled him to his feet. "He's dead, m'lord."

Asinius could only nod as he watched his men hide behind their shields, the arrows shattering against them. Screams of pain resounded in his ears as his men fell, one by one.

Joining his men in the center, he stood shoulder to shoulder with them as volley after volley kept them pinned down.

"We need to retreat," one of his officers said as an arrow pinged off his shield.

Asinius nodded, and at the top of his lungs, he shouted, "Withdraw in the double."

They reached the door separating his villa from the courtyard. A handful of arrows landed at their heels as they stumbled through.

More of his men collapsed as the multitude of arrows pinned them to the ground. The sound of battle blew through his ears like a freight train. He limped over to the cemetery beside his villa and scooped up a handful of black soil. He let out a deep sigh as he watched the dark granules fall between his fingers.

He muttered, "The hours of our lives are measured in grains of sand." He paused for a moment, said a prayer, and then prepared for his last stand.

"Make your last stand here," he said, drawing his sword across the sand.

His men lined up, some supporting their wounded comrades. There was a loud bang at the gate, and he watched it break into several pieces. The legionaries dropped the battering ram at their feet and broke through. Sandaled feet stomped through the villa and into the inner courtyard. Marus's men marched four abreast, dust floating up around their ankles.

The white tabards of Wolfryia fluttered as a light breeze blew through the yard. The legionnaires' shields butted up against one another as they marched in perfect unison. They split into two columns and surrounded Asinius and his men. Marus rode into the courtyard, his red cloak swaying in the breeze. He surveyed Asinius's men from his perched position, a smug look on his face.

"It looks like your time finally ran out, Asinius. Pity too. I thought for sure you would eventually outsmart me. But it looks like you were all show. No action as my mother used to say," Marus said.

"Brave words from a man sitting on a horse in a sea of the best warriors I trained in Dellos. Besides, your mother only said that when my fat cock wasn't in her mouth, "

Asinius said, banging his sword over the rim of his worn round shield.

Marus roared, his fingers clenching his horse's reins. "Asinius, I would love nothing more than to cut your impudent throat. But we all have orders, and mine are to extinguish your life force with torture. So, lay down your arms with your men, come quietly, and I will allow them to live," he replied, glancing at his pristine fingernails.

"My men will never surrender, and you know that. But I will surrender to you when Iceport no longer has icebergs, or perhaps when you take your tongue out of the boy's ass," Asinius hissed.

Asinius's men catcalled and jeered at their opponents as Octavius rode up from the rear of the column, his short, round frame bouncing in the saddle.

"Kill them, for God's sake," Octavius shouted as he reined in beside Marus.

Asinius swallowed his spit. "Ah, the worthless *emperor* of Wolfryia has arrived." Asinius moved his hand near his mouth, his tongue pushing out his cheek, then shouted, "Death to the aristocracy."

Asinius's men nodded at him over their shoulders and banged their swords with a responding war cry. The end had come, and even his slave Herius was armored and ready for battle. A hole in the circle opened, and Asinius walked out, Herius close on his heels.

One of the emperor's guards lifted up a crossbow to Marus. "Ah, a death wish."

He aimed and fired a bolt at Asinius's chest, but Herius leaped in front of him at the last moment, taking the blow of the quarrel.

Asinius's men rhythmically thumped their shields and pulled him behind them. A horn blew a long note from their defensive position, and his men charged out, breaking formation. The two similarly armed groups clashed throughout the courtyard.

Asinius's men were outnumbered three to one. Limbs and heads were hewn from the owners' bodies as the fight raged, both sides inflicting heavy casualties.

As the battle reached a feverish pitch, Marus watched Asinius limp into his villa, his men covering his retreat. He dismounted and sprinted to the door. After reaching it, a large man with the sandy, sun browned skin ,of a veteran with a flowing white beard shoved Marus to the ground from behind.

Spitting sand from his mouth, Marus stood up, pulled his shield into position, and extended his sword over the edge. He squared off in front of the door with his old friend Peltrasius, a legendary legionnaire in Iceport. Like many of the legionnaires from the area he had Gobo forbears,a martial tradition written in his blood. He was a pure Wolfryan, born a people forged by conquest, as diverse as the vanquished civilizations tread under the heel of empire. He was a hero, he deserved a statu,e not death, but it wasn't Marus' way to give a shit.

"Peltrasius, stand aside. My quarrel is not with you. Lay down your arms, and I will do my best to help you join my ranks. You're a good legionnaire."

Peltrasius spat on Marus's tunic, a slight smile crossing his lips. "Death first."

The two men faced off and engaged. Peltrasius lunged forward and knocked Marus to the ground again. Marus rolled over backward and stabbed up with his sword. The blow penetrated Peltrasius's armor, disemboweling him. Peltrasius fell forward, and his weight pushed Marus to the ground. They landed on the blood-soaked sand, and with great effort, Marus rolled the dead man off of him.

He pulled his sword from Peltrasius's stomach in time to see the last of Asinius's men put up a futile resistance. The wounded from the villa joined the last of their unit and fanned out in front of the door. Most were severely wounded and clung to their weapons, some barely holding on in a final act of defiance.

Marus heard their shields clink together as they formed a formation similar to that of a turtle's body.

"Forever loyal to Asinius!" shouted one of the men as they marched into the legionnaires. Shortly after the two groups engaged, Asinius's men were put to the sword.

Marus grabbed one of his men from behind and yelled, "Bring Asinius back to me—now."

He sighed and wiped his brow, checking himself for wounds. Then he glanced down and noticed he was standing on a severed arm. He picked it up and stopped one of the men walking past him.

"Does this belong to you?" Marus asked.

The legionnaire looked at him and then shook his head no.

"Ah, well, doesn't really matter. Find the owner," he said, shoving the severed arm into the man's chest.

The other legionaries with the man laughed at him as he attempted to wipe the blood off of his blue stole. Going back into the blood-drenched courtyard, Marus saw

Octavius pulling the blue stoles off of some of his dead legionnaires.

Marus walked up to him and placed his hand over his heart and bowed. "Asinius escaped," he said, barely above a whisper.

Octavius's face turned blue, his lips quivering. He turned around and stormed back to his horse. Before mounting, he turned back to Marus. "That's *one*, Prefect. Don't fail me again."

He yanked his horse's reins, turned it around, and cantered off, followed by his household guard. One of Marus's men, his red cape cut in half from the battle, sprinted to where Marus stood, scanning the villa.

"M'lord, the men are chasing Asinius down in the swamps. Will you be riding with us?" asked the man, mounting his warhorse.

"No, I will oversee the cleanup and find any treasures he may have hidden. Bring me back his head," he replied.

"And the body?" asked the man, pulling a spear stored on his saddlebag.

"Leave it for the buzzards. Just remember what I told you earlier," he said, walking back into the villa.

The legionnaire nodded and rode off, followed by the others. Marus scanned the villa and checked the walls first, the most obvious place to hide treasures. He tapped his knuckles against the wall, probing for a hollow place. The walls yielded nothing. He tossed the furniture around the room, trying to find any trap doors in the floorboards.

In frustration, he stormed back into the courtyard and over to his horse. As he was mounting, he looked at the cemetery and a newly erected cross. He stared at it for a moment and then dismounted. He pointed at one of his commanders.

"Get a shovel," he shouted.

He directed the man on what he wanted to be shoveled and then backed away. The dirt flew over the man's shoulder until he hit something metal after a few feet.

Marus's men pulled a chest out of the ground and broke the lock off of it. Marus flipped the lid open and picked up a silver goblet. There were all sorts of treasures. Coins, goblets, plates, rings, pendants, Ba warrior jewelry from the last war—a treasure trove from years of collecting.

"This must be his retirement," Marus said to his men with a chuckle. "Close it up."

"Shall we deliver it to the emperor?" asked one of his men.

"Why? He didn't find it. Return it to my quarters," he said before galloping off.

CHAPTER

Six

Goddammit, that hurt. If I get my hands on him, I'll tear him limb from limb, Viridius thought, rubbing his jaw.

Gius glanced over his shoulder, pointed at the crackling fire, and said, "If you want dinner, it's over here on the spit."

Viridius pushed himself up from the tree he was lying against and mumbled, "That's the second time you knocked me out. It won't happen again. The way you hit still proves you're a pussy."

Gius walked over to Viridius and chuckled. He knelt and cut his bindings off, then gently touched Viridius on the shoulder.

"If you want to live forever, you can leave now. I won't judge you. *Or,* you can join us, and we can dispose of Emperor Octavius together," he said.

Viridius got to his feet. "Wake up, Gius, the Rebellium is dead, and so are the people who wanted to fight in it," he shouted.

"Alecta would tell you to help us," Gius hissed.

Before Gius could get his hands up to protect himself, Viridius had him on the ground. Two punches broke Gius's nose before he knew he had been hit. He felt Viridius's large hands around his throat as if he were a chicken going to the pot.

Gius's face turned blue, and with his last ounce of energy, he brought his arms up and slammed them down across the inside of Viridius's elbows. As Viridius's grip loosened, Gius gasped and smashed the top of his head into Viridius's nose, breaking his in turn.

Viridius reared back and held his nose as Gius grabbed a branch lying nearby and swung it into his side. He fell over with a loud groan, then rolled away. Gasping in pain, he sat up and coughed as he pushed his nose back into place.

Viridius fixed his cold stare on Gius. "If you talk about my wife again, I'll kill you. Then I'll kill everything you love—"

"Everything I love?" Gius yelled over him. "They are all *dead*, you selfish prick. Can you think of anything else or only *your* dead wife?" With tears in his eyes, Gius stared at him frostily, then spoke. "They raped and murdered my turtledove, Clovia. Fucking bastards left her hanging from a tree we planted in front of our villa. My children were burned *alive* as they held me in chains to watch. Octavius ordered your wife's and my family's death because we believed in the Rebellium. We lost many of its friends of all ages to kill Tiberius. Your father and brother paid the ultimate price because they believed. I know you can continue the struggle for them." He snatched Viridius by the arm. "Help me rid Dellos of Octavius and the Wolfryian aristocracy," he said, his eyes pleading.

"I don't give a shit about your wife or your kids. My motive to kill Octavius will be for coin and coin alone. That's what I'm loyal to. Alecta . . . Alecta is just a memory now. If you want him dead, it's going to cost you and the Rebellium more than you may be willing to pay," Viridius declared.

Gius went to respond, and Viridius held his hand up. "They'll just put another tyrant in his place, and you of all people should know that. Does it really look like I give a shit about the politics of Wolfryia? If I risk my neck for you, it will be my self-preservation that does it, not my honor," he said.

"You're a cowardly fuckin' bastard," Gius shot back.

Viridius laughed. "A coward? No, I'm an opportunist."

"You killed your brother and father," Gius stated.

"Sure did. They were the *real* traitors, so I have no regrets."

Gius frowned, clearly disgusted with Viridius's attitude. "So, how much for you to sell your sword hand and your soul then?"

"It'll cost you a hundred thousand gold pieces. And not that Wolfryian shit with Octavius's face on it," he said.

Gius nodded. "Follow me to my camp, and you'll be paid."

"And where's that?" Viridius asked.

Gius smiled. "Hidden on the border between West Drathia and the Lava Lands."

Viridius chuckled. "That makes sense. Well, I'm heading back to Pistoryum for the time being. Go get my money and a plan on how to infiltrate Iceport. When you get all that together, you will find me there," he said, getting up and mounting the mule.

"You sure about that?" Gius asked.

"You have no one else, so, yeah, I'm sure."

"We *could* find another assassin," Gius shouted.

Viridius tapped the mule's flank with his ankles and rode off into the woods. He hollered over his shoulder, "No, Gius, you can't. If you could, you wouldn't have come for me."

"Expect me within a fortnight," Gius shouted at his back.

If Viridius heard him, he didn't show it.

Gius mounted his horse shaking his head with a slight smile and cantered off in the other direction. A few minutes later, Viridius came trotting back as fast as the mule would ride.

Gius laughed, then yelled, "Change of heart?"

Trotting awkwardly past him, bouncing in the saddle, Viridius said, "Yea, something like that."

Gius smiled and glanced over his shoulder. The horsemen that changed Viridius's mind came bursting through the undergrowth, whipping their steeds.

Gius spat and shouted, "Damn luck I have . . . giddy-up!"

He slammed his ankles into his horse's flanks and followed Viridius into the woods on the other side of the clearing. Gius's horse followed the donkey down the path running along the water's edge. They rode as fast as they could, glancing back occasionally to see how fast the horsemen were gaining on them. And after a few moments of riding, they knew they couldn't outrun the bounty hunters.

Viridius looked over at Gius and cut his eyes at another path further in the underbrush. Gius nodded and cut a hard left at the fork in the road. Two of the men followed Gius as Viridius spun around in the saddle and faced the other two men who had overtaken his mule on the hidden path.

This is gonna hurt, Viridius thought.

He held his arms out and propelled his body forward off the back of the mule. He clotheslined the men off their mounts and then tumbled onto the muddy, rock-filled road.

Landing on his back, he shouted in pain as his tailbone struck the hardened earth. His attackers lay on their backs, dazed and gasping. Viridius sat up and saw his sword lying next to him. He snatched it as one of the men tackled him and pinned him to the ground.

"You bastard. I'm gonna carve my money out of you if it's the last thing I do," the man said, holding a knife to Viridius's throat.

Viridius swallowed hard and then lifted himself up with the bottom of his feet. He hurled the man over his shoulders as the other attacker came up from behind him. The man pulled Viridius to his feet, punched him in the face, spinning him in the opposite direction, and then wrapped his arms around him in a bear hug.

Annoyed by the man's lack of professionalism, Viridius stomped on the man's foot and broke his toes. As the man reached for his aching foot, Viridius grabbed him by the neck, pulled it over his shoulder, and dropped down to the road. The force of the blow broke the man's neck, and he crumbled to the ground, his teeth scattering across the dirt path.

Viridius watched as the other man ran for his mount in a panic. He tripped, crawled, and stumbled toward his black warhorse. The horse spooked and bolted into the water, leaving the man stranded.

Winded from his sprint, the man put his hands on his knees and took deep breaths. After a few breaths, the merc knelt and held his hands up. Viridius paused, let the man catch his breath, and then smiled.

"You okay?"

The merc nodded with a gap-toothed smile. "Aye, you letting me go?"

"Oh yes." Savagely, Viridius cut the man's arms off at the elbows. The man screeched for a few moments, then Viridius swung the blade down and severed his head. Blood splashed across Viridius's face and arms as the attacker's head rolled to the water's edge.

Shit. Gius, he thought. He ran for the hill and considered, *Why do I even care?*

Viridius's conscience answered for him. His nagging greed always got the better of him. He sighed, shook his head, and sprinted up the hill, tripping a few times as he made it to higher ground. He crested the ridge and saw Gius placing the dead men's arms over their chests.

Humming to himself, he laid gold coins over their eyes for their trip with the boatman to the next life.

"You know something, Gius. If I didn't know you any better, I would say you're trying to kill me," Viridius said, walking up to him.

Gius grunted and sniffed loudly. "Damn sinuses."

He wiped his nose with his tunic sleeve. "A hundred thousand coins for your help, eh?" he asked.

"Yea, that's the price." He shoved his finger in Gius's chest. "But when we get to your shitty little hole, you better have my money, or I'll kill every one of you for the headache you've caused me," Viridius said.

Gius shrugged and walked away.

Viridius walked back down the hill and over to the pond to wash away the blood smeared on his hands and face. A shadow loomed over him while he washed his face in the ice-cold water. He glanced up, and a horse nudged him with his muzzle. Viridius fell back on his ass and laughed for a moment. He struggled to his feet and inspected the horse. Its coat was a brilliant jet black with white spots circling its eyes. He checked the undercarriage and winked at the horse.

"I'll name you Whispers on account of these woods, not 'cause of that," he said, glancing down as the horse nudged his hand.

For the first time in a long time, Viridius felt something other than hatred. He didn't have a soul in the world he liked, but the horse made one. He searched him for wounds.

"Nothing that won't heal, eh, Whispers?" he said quietly, touching at the scrapes from the briar patches.

Viridius led the horse to round up the rest of the animals and bodies. He found the mule and the other horses wandering down by the pond.

Picking up their reins, he brought them over to his saddle and tied them off. He mounted Whispers and rode back to where Gius was. Whispers trotted up and snorted at Gius, chomping at the bit. Gius put his arm out, palm facing it, and raised his index and middle finger. The horse neighed and pawed at the ground.

"Easy, Gius, you're worth less than the horse. I'll eat you before I eat him," he said, pushing Gius aside with the horse's flank.

Gius stared at the horse and then pushed it aside as he mounted his own.

Viridius urged Whispers forward toward the road and waved to Gius. "Keep up."

The pair rode south along the only road that ran through Batopia, known as Smugglers' Roe. The overgrown paths slowed them to a crawl, and at one point, they had to dismount to lead the animals through the obstacles in the forest.

I could get used to this, Viridius thought as he watched the red, green, and gold leaves fall onto their shoulders as they passed through.

"Careful, Viridius. We are passing through the Datta's territory now," Gius said, studying every branch blowing in the wind.

A gutted bloody body hung from a tree limb over the middle of the road, its entrails burned. It had been there for some time, and Viridius could only guess why the man was there in the first place.

As if answering his thoughts, Gius whispered, "Some things are better left unanswered."

"These guys are serious," Viridius said, staring into the underbrush.

As he spoke, two men dressed only in loincloths stepped onto the road with blowguns at their sides. Viridius and Gius reined in their horses and stopped a few feet away from them. One of the men shouted at them in a foreign language, raising his hands in a grandiose fashion. Gius raised one hand, and with the other, he pulled a torn flag from his saddlebag and held it aloft.

The man softened his tone and walked up to Gius's horse, palm out. Gius reached into his saddlebag and pulled out a burlap sack tied off at the end. He said something in their native language and handed them the bag. The men slipped back into the hedge and disappeared as quickly as they appeared.

"What did you say to them?" Viridius asked.

"I told them you were my prisoner and an enemy of the Rebellium." He closed his saddlebag. "Ain't far from the truth," Gius said, galloping out of the woods.

Viridius stopped at the edge of the forest. He stared straight ahead, not looking at Gius. The rain started down with quick bouts of thunder.

"The gods are not pleased," Gius said, pulling his cloak tighter.

"There are no gods, Gius. Just wind chimes. Now, I need supplies and armor because my chest piece is still in your damned room. And who knows what we're going to run into on the road," Viridius said.

"We can make it to my camp," Gius said, pulling his horse's reins.

Viridius snorted and pulled Gius's horse's bridle back toward himself. "Gius, we got no chance with what we have, and you know that. We got lucky with those mercs."

Gius sighed and clenched his fists. "You're right. Where to?"

"We ride for East Drathia. The black market there is as good a place as any for quality armor," Viridius said, not waiting for him to respond.

"Ah, shit. I hate Drathia," Gius said.

Gius followed behind him as the forest thinned out little by little and then turned into rolling meadows. The Kingdom of East Drathia was known to house exiled murderers who escaped the hangman's noose in Iceport and Sorra. With no real laws, it was the villagers' job to kill the rule-breakers. It was a hard place and an unusually cold place. All the rivers were frozen, and the livestock was small and scarce.

East Drathians didn't take kindly to strangers entering their lands. They posted pickets every mile or so down the only road into the major city, Vitadruma. The city was the black-market capital on the eastern seaboard of Dellos. Iceport was beautiful, the Lava Lands were deadly, and Vitadruma was the place where anything could be had for a price.

It was the only major city in Drathia. The villages and hamlets scattered throughout the barren wasteland were mostly deserted, the inhabitants willing to give up their meager huts to put food on the table by working in Iceport. A batch of eggs in Iceport was, at most, a silver coin. The same batch of eggs in East Drathia was a gold coin at the very least.

East Drathia was at least habitable, but the other half of the kingdom known as West Drathia, or the Lava Lands, was a volcanic wasteland with deep craters and volcanoes that could quickly blanket the other half if they exploded.

The Ba inhabited the Lava Lands and killed all outsiders if they dared venture in. The once-proud tribes were forced to live in exile. Nearly wiped out by Tiberius in their entirety, a few select tribes survived. After the extermination, less than a thousand were scattered throughout the inhospitable wasteland.

The Ba dealt in flesh as a currency system. The more opulent the slave, the more money they were worth. Common, everyday people in the villages were easy prey for the slavers but didn't provide the most money. The wealthy aristocracy in Iceport was worth a thousand malnourished peasants.

Viridius leaned over to Gius. "Hope you brought a plate to put over your back. It's a beautiful place where the meadows run forever, but the rivers used to run red with blood, and now they're frozen in time."

"I've been in this shitty kingdom before," Gius said with a hint of sarcasm.

A rat, the size of a small dog, scurried across the road in front of them. "Disgusting place. I usually send other men in here to do our business."

"It's a cesspool of garbage, all right," Viridius said with a laugh. "They're my kind of people, though. Just remember you could find a knife in your back by nightfall. Hell, it might even be me," Viridius said, concentrating on the shrubbery around him.

Small red eyes peered at them through the darkness as they continued their journey. They followed the road for several days as it wound its way deeper into the wilderness. They saw the occasional village but dared not stop in an attempt to mitigate any hostile encounters. Trash and both human and animal shit lined the road as they continued. The rains pounded them as they approached Vitadruma. They crossed over a hill and saw several iron spires looming above the city as they rode closer. They approached a wooden palisade with several large sections missing, the rain cascading over their shoulders.

"Why not just put a white picket fence up?" Gius muttered more to himself than Viridius.

Viridius nodded for him to go in between the gaps.

"Why me?" Gius asked.

"'Cause you're paying to kill Octavius, not to get a spear in the back. Now, chop-chop."

With a sigh, Gius pulled his cloak in tighter, dismounted, and stepped between the loose stakes. A spear flashed at the nape of his neck from behind the wall as he stepped through.

"A white picket fence won't keep the wolves away from our doors, animal or human, m'lord. What be the rich wantin' with us then, eh? Hands up, slow and steady," said the picket, pushing his spear closer to Gius's jugular.

Gius raised his hands and put them on top of his head. Viridius pushed Whispers in closer and swiftly pulled a thin blade from his boot. He put it to the guard's throat with a simple flick of the wrist.

"Watch your knife, m'lord," the guard said, glancing into the tree line.

Guards in Vitadruma could be bought for a few coins by a shady merchant to protect the city from marauders. A mercenary crossbowman with an excellent trigger finger could put a quill through the center of a man's back in the blink of an eye from a hundred yards away. Viridius looked around for any traps and not sensing anything, he turned his attention back to the guard.

"Don't make idle threats. But now that I have your attention, we need a place to sleep and the best place around here to sell some horses and buy supplies. Where can we go?" Viridius asked.

"The knife, ya lardship," said the guard, flicking his eyes at it.

"Right . . . Now, where was we?" he asked, lowering his blade.

He slid it back into his boot and urged Whispers forward to separate Gius and the guard.

The rain showers became torrential, and the wind picked up as they waited for the man to respond. Viridius held his hand up and cupped his ear, waiting for the guard to pipe up.

"The Madchester." The guard turned to face Viridius. "I can show you."

"How much?" Viridius grumbled, staring at the forest again.

"A whore. It's lonely out 'ere, m'lord."

Viridius kicked him in the face and said, "Not worth that to take us down the street. Fuck off. We'll find it ourselves."

They rode off, leaving the guard rubbing his chin. The horses' hooves could be heard clopping down the muddy road as they trotted down the enclosed alleyway.

"Hey, you all right over there?" Gius asked, poking Viridius in the side.

Viridius didn't respond or twitch a muscle. His eyes kept scanning the upper floors of the row housing for surprises until they reached the tavern. The Madchester was more a weapons house than a tavern. Blood pooled on the front stoop as a feral dog chewed on someone's discarded hand. Gius dismounted, slid his blade from its sheath, and advanced to put the dog out of its misery. Viridius snatched Gius from behind and placed his knife over his throat, drawing blood.

"Touch the dog and die. Did nothing to you. Best watch your sword hand, Gius, or I'll chop it off. You should know what I think of dogs because you know what I think of you."

Gius knew how much he cared about dogs. He'd seen him kill a few fellow legionnaires trying to kill a war dog. Viridius barked like a dog, rubbed its head as it came over, and then picked up the hand.

He threw it down the opposite alleyway and watched the dog disappear. The one thing he refused to do was kill an animal. He pushed past Gius and walked through the cheap, double wooden saloon-style doors. It felt like every eye turned toward him. Gius followed him in after tying their horses and pack animals to the post outside. He looked at the sea of unwashed faces and raised an eyebrow.

"So, you want to ask for the proprietor, or shall I?" Gius asked.

Viridius rolled his eyes and then walked over to the bar. A prostitute walked up to him and put her hand on his shoulder. She moved it to his crotch. "Fancy a 'gud time,' soldier?"

Spinning, he slapped her across the face with the back of his hand. She stumbled back and fell over a table where some of the men were gambling. The patrons stopped drinking and watched.

"Nah, you helped enough," he said, glancing down with a smile. He made eye contact with the other patrons. "Now, which of you runs the black market?" he inquired, searching for his man.

"I do," said a quiet voice from under a black, wide-brimmed hat with a white plume sticking out of the side. Viridius squinted at the person and chuckled.

"You don't sound like a man. Show me you're no eunuch," Viridius said, walking in front of him. He grabbed the soldier by the crotch and felt around for a moment.

Something ain't right here . . .

His brain registered what his hand already knew. He recoiled, but it didn't stop the aggressive onslaught that dropped him to his knees. He felt several swords press against his back, and then multiple blows from a knuckleduster mashed his nose to his face. Blood spurted across his assailant's arm as they continued to inflict pain.

Gius charged forward, freeing his sword, but two men tackled him to the floor. Viridius looked up, woozy and battered. A slight smile crossed his features showing the blood in between his teeth.

"I know a whore named Bella that hits harder than you," he said.

Four men picked Viridius up and pulled his arms behind his back. The guards pulled the pair through the tavern and threw them into the back wall, headfirst.

"Who do you work for?" the voice asked as they sat up.

"Nobody. We're just trying to sell our stuff," Viridius said.

"Tell me who sent you. Was it Fredrick the Gray?" the voice repeated.

"Never heard of him," Viridius said.

Next, Viridius felt a rope tighten around his neck. In a matter of moments, he was hanging from a crossbeam in the ceiling. His neck muscles strained as they hung him five feet off the ground. Spitting and sputtering, he swung from the rope.

"Who do you work for?" asked the voice for a third time.

"No one," Viridius said between gasps.

"I don't believe you."

"We're from the Batopia," Gius shouted into the darkness as he watched Viridius swaying.

Viridius dropped to the ground, gasping and coughing. Gius took the noose from his neck and threw it at the voice and then helped Viridius to his feet. They could hear someone walking around in the darkness behind them, the footsteps making a unique clicking sound on the floor.

"I'm the owner you're looking for," the voice said, stepping out of the shadows. "My name is Lady Corcundia of Vitadruma. I had to make sure you weren't spies of Fredrick the Gray."

"Who the hell is that?" Viridius asked, rubbing his chafed neck.

"He's the man who lives in the castle at the edge of the water." She stopped speaking for a moment and poured herself a drink and then continued. "The one that my husband, Duke Gadex of Vitadruma, once owned, but they killed him while I was away on business. I came back, and those loyal to him brought me underground, and we've been here ever since. And you are?" she asked, staring at them as she stepped further into the light.

She brought her curved cherrywood pipe to her pink lips and took a drag. Her red hair looked like someone had pulled it from a river of lava, but it was clear she lived in the underground, as dirty as it was. With a shudder, Viridius noticed her head lice.

Ugh, he thought.

The wide-brimmed hat she wore pulled over her eyes raised a little bit, and Viridius saw the faded burn marks on her face, close to her eyes. She caught him looking and pulled her hat lower.

"Name's Viridius," he said and then pointed at Gius. "That's Gius, and like we said, we're just looking to sell our pack horses and spare weapons. I need to buy some quality armor from you, and then we'll be on our way."

Corcundia didn't speak for a moment. She motioned to one of her men to head to the bar.

"Follow me. I will sort you out with what your selling," she said, pointing at the bar.

"And the armor I can buy, right?" Viridius asked as he walked toward the bar.

She nodded as a man lifted a trap door in the floorboards. The man handed Corcundia a torch and stepped aside. They descended into the darkness, the stairs creaking on their way down.

CHAPTER

Seven

Asinius ran across the wooden floorboards of his villa as the battle outside intensified. He heard Peltrasius roar as he covered the door. Asinius's spare armor had been neatly packed in a bag with food and other supplies that he was going to need for his journey. The only problem was that he didn't know where he was going.

He fastened his leather pack to his sword blade and crawled out the window. He looked across the field to the swampland and shook his head with a sigh. He limped across the field, trying to stay low in the high grass. He heard the howls of the emperor's dogs behind him as the sweat dripped from his brow. Not waiting to see if the large dogs were going to catch him, he kept stumbling to the swampland.

He breathed as calmly as he could, but he knew what the dogs could do if they surrounded him. He thought about the number of times he had sicced them on enemies fleeing after a battle. He tried to lift his sandals, but they had filled with squishy brown mud. The harder he tried, the more they sank into the muck. He switched tactics and flung the sandals over his shoulder and then started hobbling in the middle of the swampy causeway surrounded by poisonous snakes.

He ran further into the snake-, rat-, and alligator-infested land. The green and blue algae sat on top of the brackish water and floated around him lazily, hiding whatever nasties lurked beneath. He made it to a small group of tree stumps on an island to rest for a moment. The green willow tree branches from the trees nearby hung above him, hiding the swampland from the sun blazing above. With a sigh, he wiped his face and mouth with his forearm.

An arrow thudded into a trunk by his head as he put his sandals back on. Cursing himself for a fool, he ran to a larger tree half the size of a man and hid behind it the best he could. He pulled his pack from his sword and then threw it onto the opposite shoreline, barely clearing the water.

He would run no further. It was time to die a prefect. Wincing, he glanced at the welts on his legs from the reeds he had run through. Holding his vine branch in one hand, sword in the other, he stepped out from behind the tree and braced himself against it.

He could hear the howls and barks getting closer. The dogs darted over the hill following his scent and then dove into the water. One of them glanced up, sniffed the air, howled, and lunged forward. The algae splashed up in chunks as it bound toward him.

The six attack dogs were massive—built to kill. Wolfryian dogs were a hybrid of a wolf, hyena, and the domestic dog. They were trained to kill anything their handlers commanded them to. And a good dog trainer was usually missing a couple of digits on each hand. The dogs were easy to identify with their silver coat with black and yellow spots. Their fur was coarse, like cactus needles, and a black stripe ran down their spine. For his own pleasure, Octavius insisted their nails be sharpened with whetstones.

Twenty of the emperor's horsemen rode into the marsh behind the dogs. The first dog came within ten feet of where Asinius stood, saliva dripping from its incisors. He crouched low to the ground, his sword pressed against the inside of his foot. He winced as his bones popped from the stress of kneeling after his run.

The dog leaped—and impaled itself on his long blade. It slid down the length of it and then onto him. Asinius closed his eyes as the dog pushed him to the ground. He managed to roll the dead dog off of him in time for another dog to jump on top of him. It pinned him and lunged at his neck. He held the dog by the throat as he reached for his sword nearby, his fingers stretching as far as they could.

Suddenly, he felt something cold brush against his body as he struggled with the dog. He heard the dog yelp as it was flung off him and then went soaring through the air. A wave of alligators moved quickly by Asinius and dove into the water. Not losing a moment of precious time, he shot to his feet and splashed through the water to the opposite bank. He scaled a tree as the alligators bellowed in their hunt for the dogs.

The alligators were upon the riders and the dog handlers in only a few moments. They stood no chance against the ancient killing machines. The alligators tore legs from horse and rider alike, swallowing them in huge bites. The guards formed a semicircle and moved backward to the shoreline. They screamed as they were dragged under, fragments of their blue stoles floating to the top of the swampy water. The horses that remained bolted from the swamp and trampled the riders that stood in their way.

The guardsmen fell one by one until only a few men remained when they reached the shoreline. As the legionnaires backed up, they could hear bloodcurdling bellows behind them. Other alligators smelled the blood in the water and came to investigate.

Asinius put his hands over his ears to muffle the screams of agony. It seemed to go on for an eternity but finished in a blink of an eye. When the screams stopped, he looked around and saw the alligators had slipped back under.

They were gone as soon as they had appeared, taking whatever meat they had to the bottom of the marsh. One charcoal-colored alligator remained, resting its nostrils and eyes just above the waterline. It snorted as it stared at the one meal that had temporarily escaped. Then it slowly lowered itself under the water and swam away.

The next morning, Asinius woke up, hanging awkwardly on a tree branch. He had been a prefect for many years and had seen many people die, but he had never seen a group of alligators destroy humans like that before— bloody, intense, and disturbing. He glanced around and saw his pack undisturbed below him. As he looked for any more alligators, he felt something slimy rub against his leg. He glanced down and saw a yellow and black boa constrictor.

He kicked himself free and fell out of the tree backward and landed on his side. Dazed, he sat up and held his ribs. He saw there was no immediate danger, and his breathing returned to normal. He limped over to his pack and went back to his little island. He scanned the area as he chewed on a piece of bread. He watched the corpses of both man and beast floating around him and knew it would only be a matter of time before the alligators—or something worse—came back to eat what was left behind.

He carefully pulled the remaining pieces of men that he could reach onto the island. He found a pair of sandals on one body and a useable chest piece on another. He scooped up a dome-shaped helmet floating by and threw it on.

He grabbed as many weapons as he could carry, shouldered his pack, and then ran across the swamp to the other side. The swampland ran as far as the eye could see, a blue haze dancing above the water. He slowly made his way through the algae, stabbing the bottom of the riverbed to make sure nothing attacked him. Soon, he saw a long, twisting road ahead of him and breathed a sigh of relief.

Several days passed on his lonely journey to nowhere. His lips were dry and cracked from the lack of clean water, the corners of his mouth collecting white spit. In the distance, he spotted an area that looked to have a small river.

A tall, white picket fence surrounded a quiet farmhouse. The house sat on the edge of the pond attached to a waterwheel. With his last bit of energy, Asinius grabbed the fence and pulled himself into the yard. A young man with curly black hair ran to his side and yelled for the farm's caretaker. The old man ran to them and looked down at Asinius.

"This is an important man, Tersius. A very important man. His nails are perfect, and he has all his teeth," the man said, rapping his knuckles against Asinius's gold-inlaid breastplate.

The old man noticed a gold coin fall out of Asinius's pouch. He reached down and bit into it. "Go fetch your father."

Asinius opened one eye and raised his sword to the man's neck. "I've killed men for much less. Don't be a thief. It sets a bad example for the boy," he said.

"And how would you know what's good or ain't good for the boy?" the old man asked.

"You're right. I don't. But I do know my sword arm can sever your balls right now."

The man glanced down, swallowed hard, and nodded. Asinius tapped the man's balls with the knife he had slid from his belt. He emphasized the words after each knife stroke.

"Do I make myself clear? Set . . . a . . . good . . . example. Now, fetch me some water," he demanded.

The old man did as he was told and ran back faster than he left. He held a cup to Asinius's lips and helped him sit up. Asinius drank deeply and then spat the water up. He dry-heaved, snatched the cup from the man's hands, and took smaller sips.

Sighing, he tilted his head back and muttered, "Ah, now that's the good stuff."

Tersius's father, Primus, reached them and leveled his spear at Asinius's throat.

"Help you with something, Prefect?" he asked, inching the blade closer to Asinius's Adam's apple.

Asinius opened his eyes, cocked his head to one side, and said, "I don't recognize your face behind that beard. Who are you?"

Primus sneered and hissed, "I am Centurion Primus of West Drathia, First Leader of Alpha Legion 1. A man from your tribe, on a list you wrote for those of us loyal to the Rebellium. Come to join the cause or be killed by it?" he asked, not taking his eyes off of him.

Asinius chuckled and shook his head in disbelief. He went from being hunted by his people to landing at his enemy's feet. There was no way out now. He held his hands out in front of him. He spat on Primus's sandals. "So help the gods, I will kill you for what you're planning to do," Asinius hissed.

Primus snickered and then bound Asinius's hands. "You and what army, Prefect?" he asked. "Your loyal legionnaires are all gone now, remember?"

Primus picked him up by the throat and shoved him in the direction of the barn.

"Primus, I should have hung you when I had the chance. I guess letting you go doesn't get me any points, does it?" Asinius asked, knowing the answer.

"Nope. We may have been friends long ago, Asinius, but now I have over a thousand reasons to kill you. One for every member you had executed!" Primus shouted, smashing Asinius over the head with the pommel of his sword.

CHAPTER

Eight

Viridius, Gius, and Lady Corcundia descended the stairs and into the crudely excavated basement. She put her torch into a holder on the wall and took off her black cloak and wide-brimmed hat. Stepping up to the table, she pulled her red hair over the burns on her face. Several items on the table caught her eye as she walked around the room, smoking her pipe.

"I see you mostly have broken shit," she said, picking up a broken dagger with two fingers. She looked at it in disgust, shook her head, and then dropped it on the floor. "I'll let the rats have that one."

Gius smiled. "Lady Corcundia, we don't need much—"

"Oh, we need as much as you have. This fucker owes me a hundred thousand gold coins. He can start paying me the other ninety-nine thousand five hundred pieces later," Viridius said.

She laughed and picked up a shattered sword. "The weapons are worthless, not fit for a child to wield," she said.

"Maybe, but you can melt down the metal and remake a few," Gius piped up, hoping not to come out of pocket.

She shook her head. "We're not smiths, old man."

"OK, fine. How much to buy good quality armor?" Gius asked, trying to refrain from moving his hand to his sword pommel.

"A hundred coins," she replied, putting her hat back on.

Viridius guffawed. "What's in that pipe . . . belladonna?"

"Bellweed. I don't smoke belladonna. But that's not the point. I make the prices, and they are nonnegotiable," she said, opening a chest on the far wall with her toe.

Gius groaned at Viridius's apparent lack of negotiating skills. They needed her much more than she needed them. The thought crossed his mind that all she had to do was kill them. No one would bother looking for them either, and after carefully scanning the faces of her men, he wanted to make sure no one was thinking of surprising them. Gius butted back into the conversation, cutting off Viridius.

"Won't ask anything for the weapons then. Take them. How about you take the donkey and spare horse in trade?" Gius asked.

"OK, but I still want forty gold pieces. How does that strike your fancy?" she asked, hoisting a crude leather jerkin from the chest.

Viridius laughed as he looked at the deteriorating jerkin. "You're kidding, right? That ain't quality, that's—"

"Shit," Gius said, finishing his sentence.

"You haven't got the coins for good quality," she said, dropping the jerkin back into the chest.

"Like hell I don't," Viridius said.

He liked the woman's style; she was ballsy. He stared into her eyes for a moment and saw a flicker of pain, the same pain he carried. Losing a spouse would only be seen by those afflicted by the same loss . . . a look of solemnness, a tortured haunting of the eyes. But it wasn't a unique pain by any stretch of the imagination in Dellos. It was a cold and dreary place, even in the sunlight.

A kindred soul, he thought, glancing in her direction.

Gius nudged Viridius as he spat on the ground at her feet. "I want real armor, not some leftover piece of shit from a bygone age." Viridius paused and slid his hand to the hilt of his sword. "Come to think of it, I have a better idea. What if I just take what I want and kill you and your men?" he asked.

Corcundia smirked. "We outnumber you four to one. Can you and the old man kill eight others before being killed?" she asked, pulling her sword from its sheath, her men following suit.

Gius touched Viridius's arm and whispered, "This is not the time for pride. Pay her, get the shitty armor, and then we ride for the Rebellium," he said.

Viridius snatched the jerkin out of her hands, sniffed it, and wrinkled his nose.

"By all that's holy in Dellos, this thing looks like it's a hundred years old." He sniffed it again. "And it smells like old Wolfryian blood."

Corcundia smiled and winked. "That's the owner in the corner the rats are chewing on."

Viridius glanced over his shoulder with a disgusted look. With an exaggerated sigh, he withdrew his pouch and counted out the coins. He begrudgingly handed them to her and donned the creaking armor.

This smells like shit and feels worse.

As Viridius opened his mouth to say goodbye and good riddance . . . he froze. They heard a loud pounding knock from upstairs. One of her men ran up the stairs to investigate. Corcundia reached the main floor in time to see one of her men walking to the barred door. In a boisterous feminine voice, the man asked, "Who is it?"

"By order of Fredrick the Gray, open this door. We are here to serve an arrest warrant to Lady Corcundia. She has sold her last batch of illegal weapons. Now, surrender!" Fredrick's herald shouted.

In response, Lady Corcundia's men pulled their weapons and flipped over the tables near them for cover. She pulled her hat low over her eyes and tied her hair in a ponytail.

Corcundia spat, "Any of you bastards want to surrender?" she shouted.

"No!"

"I do. It ain't our fight. We're going out the back," Viridius said, keeping his sword sheathed as he straightened the tight-fitting jerkin.

"What, you runnin'? Always heard you were a vicious bastard in a fight," she said with a smile, loading her handheld crossbows.

"You know us?" Gius asked, an eyebrow raised.

She nodded and aimed at the front door. "You're Gius Flavius, and he's Viridius Vispanius." She pointed to the bounty posters. "Steep price on your heads. Good thing for you I hate the emperor more than the Rebellium."

"Stay here, Gius, and you'll never find me again. Your money ain't worth dying for some shitty hole in the wall," Viridius said, searching for an exit.

As they argued, Viridius held one hand up and silenced Gius. He heard a loud whining sound by the door and cocked his head to the side. It was a moment too late when he realized what was happening. He had heard the same sound once before. The proper name for the equipment that was whining was known as a Fire Horn. They were metallic instruments loaded with a substance called Hellrot that burned as hot as the sun, melting skin from bone. The device was lit at the bottom by a torch, and once lit, the machinery made a high squealing noise, and then liquid fire spewed from the opening. If it malfunctioned, the flame would vaporize everyone in a ten-yard radius.

Viridius watched a boy stroll up to the door and put his ear and hand to it. A thought flew through Viridius's mind. *Shit, it's gonna blow.*

Viridius bellowed, his voice booming off the walls. "Someone, get the bo—" He found himself running toward the door for no reason, arm outstretched. *I don't care about them, do I? Why am I running to the door?*

The explosion shook the building and set it ablaze. The boy and a few men standing next to him screeched and melted into fiery puddles. The blast launched Viridius across the room and onto a table, smashing it to pieces.

The heat coursing through the air made it almost impossible to breathe. Thick, acrid black smoke that smelled like sulfur hung high in the air around them. The explosion was so loud that several of Corcundia's men nearest the door never heard their attackers barrel in behind them. The deafened men stumbled into one another, their burnt and seared lungs holding their screams of pain as the attackers' swords and axes cut them down. Gius and Corcundia coughed violently and wiped their eyes as they tried to form a defense line with the men still standing around them.

"I can't see shit," shouted one of her men, standing near Viridius.

"Then squint," Corcundia shouted.

A tall man wearing a gray cloak stepped through the hole where the door used to be and licked his lips. To look at Fredrick the Gray, you wouldn't think he was anything special, but he was a hard, calculating, miserable man. The gate guard Viridius assaulted had run to the castle after Viridius broke his jaw and told Fredrick the whole story. Fredrick was delighted by his luck when he was informed of the assault. He could kill two birds with one stone—literally.

Looking around the room and sucking on his toothless gums, he said, "Clean this shit up. No survivors!"

Viridius held his head in his blistered hands as the screams around him got louder. A gloved hand pulled him off the ground and pushed him against the bar. Corcundia thrust a sword and shield into his hands.

"Fight or die," she shouted.

Gius limped over to them with her remaining men. Corcundia shouted above the noise, "Form ranks!"

She looked at Viridius and shouted, "One hundred gold coins to fight with us!"

"Five hundred," he replied, shoving his sword into an attacker's stomach.

Dodging a sword thrust, Corcundia elbowed a man in the face, shattering his teeth with a bone-chilling crunch. She ducked his overhand swing and drove a thin blade into the man's chin. He stumbled back as blood seeped from his mouth. She yanked the blade free and kicked him to the floor.

"Deal—now, help!" she said.

Another attacker charged Viridius, who spat in the man's face and swung his sword, severing the man's balls. Moving quickly, he cut down another three men with little effort. He saw Fredrick the Gray standing in the middle of the floor unprotected. He kicked a spear lying on the ground up to his waist and hurled it at him.

The spear flew through the air, and as it was about to skewer Fredrick, he grabbed one of his men and used him as a shield. Fredrick threw the body to the side and retreated to where his men were forming a shield wall.

Damn, Viridius thought.

With a war cry, Corcundia's remaining men charged into the attackers' shield wall and broke it open. Viridius pulled an enemy closer to him by the neck, snapped it, and held him as a shield. Several bolts from a crossbow hit his human shield in the face and torso as he advanced toward Fredrick. Viridius launched the dead man into a group of attackers as they charged him. He battled three men and dodged their blows as they pushed him back to the bar.

A man with a maul snuck behind Viridius and struck him across the back. The blow knocked him to the ground, out of breath. It sent one of his daggers clattering across the floor.

Goddammit, I'm getting slow.

He groaned as the man held the maul over his head and swung down. The blow stopped midway in its arc. The man stutter-stepped, then stumbled to the floor, the maul sliding across the floor behind him. Viridius's attacker looked surprised and yanked the quill from his stomach. He got to one knee, and another bolt hit him in the face, showering Viridius with dark blood.

Viridius glanced over his shoulder and shook his head. Corcundia nodded as she stuffed liquor bottles into the bag on her hip. She shouted, "Saving your life just cut the price in half!"

He could hear Gius laughing on his left at his misfortune. Angered, Viridius snatched his sword from the floor and joined Corcundia's forces as they retreated. She directed a few of her men to build a barrier and fight a rear-guard action. Backing up little by little, their numbers dwindled.

Corcundia ran for the stairs, but an attacker yanked her by the hair and muscled her to the ground. She held him off the best she could as he stabbed at her throat. One of her men slit the man's throat from behind, then turned around to engage Fredrick's men but was run through. Fredrick lunged at her unprotected chest with a spear.

Viridius threw a table leg at Fredrick and hit him in the temple. As he crumpled to the floor, the rest of Fredrick's men closed in. Viridius picked up Corcundia and pushed her to the back of the bar.

"Lady Corcundia, this way!" shouted one of her men, holding off another attacker.

She ran down the steps and into the basement with a handful of her most experienced men hot on her heels. Viridius reached the trap door, and someone pushed him down the steps behind her. As he fell, the beam in the ceiling above him broke free. The door slammed shut with a clang, and the beam crushed the man who closed off their escape.

With a thud and a loud groan, Viridius hit the last step and sprawled out. Panting, he looked around.

Damn, that hurt. Is this all that made it?

He counted ten men, most of them severely wounded. Screams could be heard above them as the last of her men put up a futile resistance. Corcundia ignored their screams and pushed a piece of the wall in under a torch. She wiped her temple and drew blood from her brow.

"I hate that man. I'll kill him if it's the last thing I ever do," she muttered as she pushed the door open.

Viridius walked up behind her. "Where's my money?" he asked.

"No time for that, Viridius. We have to go," Gius said.

Viridius glared at Gius and held his finger up with a shushing sound.

Corcundia cut her eyes at Viridius. "Why didn't you kill Fredrick?" she demanded.

"You didn't pay me for that."

She glanced over her shoulder and saw two of her men kneel at the foot of the stairs, spears at the ready.

"For Kooris!" they shouted.

Kooris was the God of Blood—one that demanded human sacrifices for protection. Few, if any, people in Dellos worshipped the banned god, and the penalty for the belief was to be covered with honey and left tied to an anthill, Octavius's favorite method of torture.

The wall swung open, and the group quickly ventured into the passageway. Viridius was the last to enter the passage after he found a few pots of oil by the door. He pulled the torch from the holder and placed it over them.

"Good luck, men," he said over his shoulder, shutting the door.

Corcundia led the group through the passageway as the cobwebs brushed against her face. Rats and mice scattered as she swung her torch by her feet. Her torch swung by Gius's ankles, and he noticed hundreds of skeletal bones. He stared at Corcundia, aghast.

"What the—?"

"Don't play innocent with me, Gius. This is for Kooris. She does not protect those who don't sacrifice in her honor," she said, shouldering past him.

One of her men collapsed in the tunnel as they began to move again.

"And that's another one!" she shouted as her men followed her obediently down the tunnel.

Viridius knelt next to the body. He hummed as he turned the dead man over onto his back. Viridius smiled as he closed the man's eyelids. Pulling the man's pouch from his belt, he emptied it into his. He waved Corcundia's men on until he was the last one in the tunnel. He didn't hear the explosion he was looking for, so he cupped his hand around his ear and slowed his breathing.

It should have gone off by now.

A hand grabbed his shoulder from behind, startling him. Gius pulled him back and said, "Put that money back, you worthless thief. You're someone else now. Not the man I remember."

Viridius grabbed him by the throat and slammed him into the wall. "Watch yourself, asshole. You came looking for me, remember?" Pointing down at the body, he said, "Guy's dead. He ain't going to need it."

Viridius shook off Gius's grip and then tossed the empty pouch to Gius with a snort. "I work for gold—the same as you."

"What did you just say to me, thief?" Gius asked, advancing with his sword drawn.

"Watch your sword, or you'll never draw one again," Viridius said, picking up the dead man's sword. "You steal dreams, and I steal gold. Same shit pile, just a different dog. We're both slaves and always will be," Viridius said.

Gius clenched his teeth and grumbled something under his breath.

Viridius laughed boisterously, then spat on the body. "What do ya know? He's still dead. Besides, I closed his eyes, didn't I? He never saw a thing. I do have *some* class."

The argument ended, and a light could be seen down the tunnel. They heard footsteps approaching, accompanied by small shadows. Gius pushed Viridius down the tunnel and shouted, "Go!"

An explosion finally broke the silence and sent a ball of fire hurtling down the shaft. The force from the oil bombs Viridius built shifted the wooden beams in the tunnel. Screeches of terror and fear were heard for a moment— then nothing but darkness. Gius ran as fast as his broken toe would let him as the dirt and debris fell from the sides of the tunnel. He caught up with Viridius as the tunnel collapsed with a loud creak. They leaped the last few feet and rolled into the daylight.

Laughing could be heard above them as they brushed the debris from their scalps and clothes. Corcundia and her men held their horses' reins. Viridius stood up and walked over to stroke Whisper's mane, then touched his forehead to his muzzle.

To hell with the Rebellium. Got this horse. That's all I need.

Viridius glanced at Corcundia and said, "Where the hell are we?"

"Under an overhang, south of the city," she said.

Gius brushed himself off again. "Where will you go now, Lady Corcundia?" he asked.

"Not sure." She took a deep breath. "I think I'll gather more men and go back to kill Fredrick the Gray."

"We could use your help to get to our headquarters, and if you're interested, killing the emperor," Gius said, mounting his horse.

Corcundia stared at the faces of her men and then back to Gius and asked, "What's the pay?"

"We'll pay you ten thousand coins for your help," Gius said.

Corcundia nodded. "Deal. It'll cost you more for my leadership when we kill that piece of shit, Octavius."

Gius gave a quick head nod. "I'll speak to the council when we arrive."

The small group rode down the road in single file, occasionally glancing over their shoulders.

Viridius saw riders on the horizon. "Seems someone's coming our way." He counted their group. Eight, including himself, were all that were in fighting shape.

Thirty riders wearing red tunics over light chain mail rode over the hill and spread out across the road. They galloped down the slope, weaving in and out of the trees in their path.

Viridius motioned for his group to lead their horses into the trees lining the roadway. The riders stopped where Viridius's group was hidden and spoke for a moment. They watched the soldiers dismount, all except a man mounted on a chestnut-colored mare. Viridius leaned against a tree and bit into an apple.

"They're coming too fast. We need to form a battle line," one of the men shouted.

The other riders formed a line, their spear tips gleaming in the sunlight.

"Hold the line!" one of the men shouted to his comrades.

Viridius watched as the second group of riders came over the hill, riding hard. The other group urged their horses into the spear wall, and as the two groups collided, the riders exploded through the defensive line. Screams and curses from the wounded and dying cracked the crisp, cold, silent air.

The man on the chestnut mare was knocked unconscious as he fought an attacker. The aggressor raised his sword over the man's head to finish him. One of the unconscious man's companions dove over his body and absorbed the blow. The shiny sword stuck in the sacrificial man's rib cage, preventing him from attacking further.

Viridius heard a voice shout, "Cheap Wolfryian steel!"

The man put his boot on the body and yanked at his sword hilt. After a moment, he gave up and pulled a backup blade to finish the job. Viridius could hear himself suck in his breath.

That worthless bast—

Fredrick the Gray's burnt cloak fluttered in the wind. Viridius bent over and attempted to pull a knife from his boot. As he rose to his feet, he felt two elbows lay across his back and push him back down.

"Do . . . not . . . move," Corcundia said, accentuating her words.

Viridius could hear two crossbow bolts release and fly downrange. One bolt hit Fredrick in the shoulder, and one missed.

"Damn the gods. Guess it's going to be the old-fashioned way," Corcundia said, using her blade to lift a branch in front of her out of the way.

She stepped out onto the road and rolled her sleeves up.

"You bitch, I'll kill you for that," Fredrick spat.

Corcundia smiled and settled into a defensive stance, her legs shoulder-width apart. The men that remained with her charged out of the tree line to aid the riders in red. Fredrick roared and charged her, pushing a man in his path out of the way.

Corcundia sidestepped as Fredrick flailed wildly. She paused, stared Viridius in the eye, winked, and then buried her blade to the hilt in Fredrick's neck as she dodged another of his overhand swings. He let out an animalistic screech and desperately reached for the hilt as he made loud, choking sounds.

Whispering in his ear, she said, "You rotten bastard. That's for my husband."

She kicked him to the ground as the mysterious men in red that were fighting with them cleaned up the remainder of Fredrick's troops. Viridius's allies ran to their leader and carried him into the tree line. Gius pulled his blade from his opponent's back and wiped the sweat from his brow.

Without being asked by Viridius, he said, "In case you're wondering, the man in red they're waking up is the King of Tramonia, a fella by the name of Aksutamoon."

"I've heard of him. What's he doing in Drathia?" Viridius asked.

"Knowing his reputation, I would say making sure his shipment of wine doesn't go missing," Gius said.

The Tramonian soldiers dragged a body past them while they talked.

"And him?" Viridius asked, his eyes following the body.

"The de—I mean the wounded man is Prince Katsootamun."

Viridius stared at the man's ashen face, his gray tongue hanging out. "Gius, that guy is dead as a rat in a trap."

Gius sighed. "He is the heir . . . well, *was* the heir to the Tramonian crown."

Viridius laughed. "So much for the gentry. Should have learned how to use a sword, not his body to protect someone."

Gius bit his lip.

"What are you thinking about? How to pay me?" Viridius asked.

"If we could somehow get them to join the Rebellium, we may just have a chance against Octavius," Gius said.

"A king join your silly *cause*? Fat chance. I'm only coming because the money is good." He pointed at the unconscious king. "He don't need money. He's rich enough to finance his own wars. But I'm sure if you pucker up, his lardship will love you for it," Viridius said, moving his tongue inside his cheek as he worked his hand by his mouth. With a sinister laugh, he clapped Gius on the back, turned around, and disappeared into the shadows.

CHAPTER

The freezing green water cascaded across Asinius's face. Sputtering, he screamed as he looked at his shoulder joints, separating from his arms as they hung above his head. He spat out the slimy water that had slid into his mouth and gagged. He had been hanging with his arms tied above his head for hours. His fingertips had turned white, and he had the feeling of pins being stuck into his arms and shoulders. The pain worsened by the second, and it felt like every ligament and muscle he had were ripping from their sockets.

Primus towered over him, the empty water pail in his hand. With no remorse, he kicked Asinius in the ribs over and over. With a smug and sinister look, he whispered, "Who loves ya, Prefect?" He sent another score of kicks into Asinius's rib cage. "Say it."

Asinius growled and lowered his head. "You do."

"Damn right," Primus said, continuing the barrage of fists and stomps to his body.

Asinius screamed for mercy.

Primus giggled and said, "You showed no mercy to us. You killed women and children—innocents . . . and now you will pay the price," he shouted, wagging his finger near Asinius's mouth.

Asinius waited patiently and then bit down with all the force he had. Howling in pain as blood dripped from his missing fingertip, Primus held his hand in his opposite palm and began to kick Asinius in the ribs.

"You son of a whore!" Primus shouted.

Pushing the heel of his shit-stained boot onto Asinius's rotator cuff, he pushed down until he heard a pop. Asinius spat out the finger and screamed in pain.

"You bit my finger off, you—"

"Piss on you. It's easy to lay blame on your old leader, isn't it? You were all fools to rise against him. Every one of you should have been executed," Asinius shouted over him, blood dripping from his lower lip.

Boiling with rage, Primus hissed through clenched teeth, "My uncles and many others died to give us freedom. You sold us out because of misplaced *loyalty*. So, where is your emperor now, you worthless rat?"

"Take these bindings off and call me a rat. The problem with you, Primus, is you believe that shit about your *cause* and what it supposedly represented. Not what it really was. Lies—it was all lies. It was a group of people who wanted nothing more than anarchy. There will *always* be an emperor; *that* is the only truth."

Using one finger at a time, Asinius held them up. "There are three truths in life, Primus. You're an ignorant asshole, so I'll explain them. One, taxes are always due. Two, *loyalty* is just another word for services rendered. And lastly, death comes for us all. And I'll be there for yours."

"You haven't changed a bit. You're still an arrogant, patronizing asshole," Primus said, pulling a blade sheathed against his forearm.

Primus placed the blade against Asinius's throat, and with an ice-cold menacing stare, he started to choke him. Asinius gasped and fought to free his hands as he began to asphyxiate. Tersius ran into the room and pulled on Primus's shoulder.

"Riders!"

Primus held his grip for a few more seconds and then withdrew. Smiling, he head-butted Asinius and knocked him unconscious. Primus ran to the barn window and saw the farmhand meet the men at the gate.

"Shit. Wolfryians. They must be here to claim him. Tersius, get the horses ready and tie him to a saddle. He must be brought to council to stand trial," Primus said.

"What about you?"

Checking his swords, Primus said, "I'll hold them off as long as I can. You know where you're going. Find Uncle Gius and tell him what happened." Pointing at Asinius, he said, "Under no circumstance are you to let him go free. Give him to the first Rebellium soldier you see. Never return to this house. Tell me that you understand."

Tersius teared up and sniffed. Primus snatched him by the chin and punched him across the face.

"Toughen up, boy. We all die, and I've lived long enough. Those are real legionnaires out there—not the ones from your nightmares. They'll flay the skin from your body and drink from your skull—or worse. Get the man on the horse and ride, son. And—"

"Then you'll follow, right?" Tersius asked, grasping his shoulder.

Primus chuckled. "No, do . . . not . . . look . . . back," he emphasized, squeezing his shoulder.

Tersius nodded, his lower lip quivering. Primus unsheathed one of his swords and thrust it into the boy's shaking hands and said, "This is the sword carried by every man in our family back to the beginning. Keep it sharp, and it will keep you alive."

The guards shouted at the man outside, interrupting Primus. Tersius winced as Primus turned his face back to his. Softly, he said, "Tersius, go now and let me die the way all men should."

A tear fell from Tersius's eye, and he quietly asked, "And how is that?"

With a grin, Primus said, "Free, boy. Always free."

Tersius stared at him, blinking back tears and then hugged him around the neck. Primus patted him on the back and pointed to the horse and said, "Remember how we face death. Go."

Curses of pain could be heard out front as the battle began. Primus stood and cracked his back and neck. With a smile at the corner of his mouth, he waved to Tersius as he galloped off. He watched him ride off over the hill and then turned toward the door. Primus watched his hired farmhand cut down two of the men, and then a guard speared him through the spine. The man looked down his chest, touched the spear tip, and then collapsed. Primus knelt and began to make small incisions on his hand, whispering:

For the cowards, the faithless and the detestable,
For the murders, the immoral and the innocent,
For the liars, cheats, and thieves,
The dying and the dead . . .
Forgive people like me.

Finishing his prayer, he silently pushed the barn doors open and mounted his horse. He crouched low in the saddle as the legionnaires came to the door.

"Long live the Rebellium!" he roared, slamming his ankles into his horse's flanks.

His horse lurched forward . . . and was cut down, throwing him from the saddle. He rolled to his feet and drove his sword through two men until a spear pierced the back of his thigh.

"Where is Asinius? We know you helped him escape," shouted the legionnaire holding the spear.

"I should have given him to you, but the honor of his execution falls to the Rebellium." He spat at their feet, pulled his knife from his arm sheath, and launched into a man's throat standing in front of him. The man gasped and clutched his bloody throat and then fell to his knees. Primus laughed maniacally until spears entered both of his shoulders from behind and pinned him to the red and brown dirt. He grunted in pain as they pulled their swords.

"Free—" He whispered, but his words were cut short as his throat was slit.

Aksutamoon, the king of Tramonia, woke up a few hours later by a roaring fire. Overweight, with sickly light olive brown, speaking of too much loafing and not enough exercise, he looked more like a swollen red apple than a king. His men had washed the blood from his face, revealing his battered countenance. The king had an upset stomach, and his large ears wouldn't stop ringing. He groaned and lifted his head, yawning to pop his ears.

"Katsootamun," he shouted.

No one spoke.

He shouted louder as he cleared his throat and spat, "Katsootamun!"

Lady Corcundia came to his side as he struggled to get up. "Are you in pain, King Aksutamoon?"

He glanced up and smiled. "Lady Corcundia of Vitadruma, what on Dellos are you doing here?"

"Until last night, still selling black market goods. But Fredrick burned my inn down. I heard you were captured and being transported back to Iceport for crimes against the empire. Any truth to that?" she asked, one of her eyebrows lifting.

He nodded and sat up. "Wolfryia ain't my empire. I sell my wines to whoever the hell I feel like selling them to. Octavius doesn't own us. I'm a Tramonian, and you know we bow to no man. And, yes, I was captured. Fredrick's men ambushed us as we rode for Batopia. He confiscated our shipment, saying it could only be sold in Wolfryia."

He continued, "That raggedy bastard imprisoned us a few months ago. He sent a courier to get a ransom, but my cousin told them he wouldn't pay. My cousin,

Tatootamoon, is a greedy bastard and wrote me off for dead. They were bringing us to the town square for execution when our escort sprinted toward your inn. We escaped, and they caught us here. It was too easy to escape. I wonder why that is."

Gius piped up behind him, "That's because of me and him, Your Eminence," he said, pointing over to where Viridius was sitting cleaning his nails. "If you want revenge, I can guarantee that I can make it happen."

"How's that?" Aksutamoon asked.

Nodding in Viridius's direction, Gius said, "Let him do it. I know you have no love loss for the empire. And the Rebellium could use your help when we take Iceport from Octavius's greedy, blood-soaked hands. What do you think?" Gius asked, sitting next to him by the fire to warm his hands.

"What can your man do my army can't do?"

Leaning toward the fire, Gius whispered, "An army during a siege is destroyable." He held up his index finger and winked. "But one man, Your Highness, one man is always expendable."

Aksutamoon smiled and glanced over Gius's shoulder. He saw something on the side of the road on a pyre of stones surrounded by chopped wood. He held his hand over his brow and said, "Who's that?"

No one answered him.

"I said, who the hell is that over there?"

Viridius walked up to him and said, "Your dead brother, Kaksoota, or some damn thing. I found his sword unused, so I'm keeping it. And this chain mail," he said, feeling the notches cut into the sword with his index finger.

"But you can have his worthless boots and his tattered, stinky clothes. His feet were too small anyway," he said, dropping the boots in the dust.

Aksutamoon shook uncontrollably, his face turning a deep red.

"One question, though. Was your brother the village idiot? I mean, with all due respect, why carry a notched sword, known for breaking blades, and then use your body for a shield?" Viridius turned around and shrugged his shoulders. "Hell with it; he's better off dead. More coin for me . . . I mean us," Viridius said, picking up Katsootamun's coin purse from the ground.

Gius put his fingers to his temples and groaned. He rubbed them slowly and muttered, "Dammit, Viridius."

Gius watched as Aksutamoon jumped to his feet. Gius rushed to him and held him under the arms. He attempted to hold him back until the others could assist in restraining him.

Viridius laughed and bit into an apple, "What . . . What did I say?"

Aksutamoon shouted, "I'll murder you. If it's the last thing I do, I'll murder you."

Viridius raised his hand and spread two fingers out in front of him and blew a raspberry. A large, bluish vein popped out from the center of Aksutamoon's forehead. He pulled several men with him until they brought him down in a cloud of dust at Viridius's feet.

Viridius dropped the apple core on Aksutamoon's forehead with a sigh and said, "Forget I said anything. I got emperors to kill and money to make. Got no time for fake barbarian kings that drink piss wine."

The color drained from Aksutamoon's face as Viridius walked away whistling. Aksutamoon looked around, ran his hand through his hair, and pulled a blade hidden near the nape of his neck. His men lined up four abreast and waited for the order to give chase. He opened his mouth, but his throat closed on him.

A voice boomed in his head, "*Leave him be. Burn your brother's corpse if you want to see the sun tomorrow. Killing Viridius will bring you no peace.*"

Aksutamoon fell to his knees, choking.

Gius ran to his side and shouted, "Help, he's choking."

His men sprinted to his side, but he waved them off. They looked at him suspiciously but obeyed. From behind a tree, Lady Corcundia lowered her clenched fist and shook her wrist out. She groaned and slumped against the tree, exhausted. Beads of sweat dripped from her brow, and her blue eye with a yellow pupil twitched as a tear of blood fell from the corner of it.

Aksutamoon took a deep breath, trying to clear his throat. He coughed harshly as his men rushed to pull him to the fire and pour water down his throat. Corcundia watched Viridius walk away and smiled.

"Your allies will protect you long before you know we are there," Corcundia muttered.

As she walked out from the tree line, Gius stared at her. She nodded in his direction and walked up to Aksutamoon.

"I step away to piss, and you look like death. What the hell happened?"

He rubbed his throat awkwardly and said, "Allergies. Mind your business."

She smirked and rolled her eyes.

Aksutamoon growled at her and stood up. Spitting into the fire, he pushed her aside and walked over to his brother's funeral pyre. Without ceremony, he threw a torch onto his body. As the embers from the fire spewed heavenward, black smoke rose from the pyre. The fire raged on the pyre for a few moments, and then Aksutamoon lifted his head. He slammed a bastard sword into the rough clay and then shoved his brother's helmet on it.

Gius walked up to Corcundia. "Missed a spot, m'lady." Corcundia's blue eye turned a deeper shade as she clenched her fist. "Easy, Witch, only I know," Gius said.

"Know what?" she asked, raising an eyebrow.

Gius stopped walking and motioned for her to follow him. "You're a Blood Wizard, aren't you?"

Corcundia bristled. "And if I am?" she asked.

Gius spread his hands. "Oh, no problems here. You could really help us with our rebellion," he smiled. "Is it true, you lose a year of your life when you use your ability?" he asked.

She walked back to the tree line. "It's worth the price to play the part of a goddess."

A few hours later, while everyone slept, Gius and Aksutamoon talked by the dying fire. "I'm sorry about what happened with Viridius, Your Emine—"

"Shut up," Aksutamoon hissed, staring at Viridius's back while he slept.

With a quick glance over his shoulder, Aksutamoon waved one of his men over. "Kill him, Trakuta, and then carry the body away. Chop him up and leave him for the vultures."

He looked over at Gius and said, "Your assassin's life ends today."

"E—" Gius shouted.

He fell into the dirt from the solid blow that hit him from behind. Trakuta pulled his blade and rotated the hilt backward in his palm as he crept through the camp. He was as slim as a reed with green tattoos on his face that had faded as he aged.

His red goatee was starting to gray, but his eyes were still as sharp as a tack. He tugged his ratty hood back and tossed it at his feet. As he came near Viridius's fire, he could hear him snoring. Trakuta sat on his heels in the shadows for what seemed like an eternity . . . then he made his move.

His knife hit Viridius's back and made the sound of a lead pipe hitting a brick oven. Viridius rolled into Trakuta's shins and knocked him off balance. He snatched Trakuta's testicles and gave a swift tug. Trakuta was a powerful assassin, but no match for Viridius's viselike grip. He howled, waking the camp as Viridius got to his knees and yanked his sack upward again. Trakuta shrieked in pain as Viridius released his balls and then grabbed his penis.

"You're a good assassin. I can't kill a professional, so I'll let you live," Viridius whispered, then headbutted him across the bridge of his nose, breaking it.

Viridius let him go, kicked him behind the knee, and knocked him down. He slammed the cast-iron plate attached to his back across Trakuta's that he had hidden in the folds of his cloak. Aksutamoon stalked toward him with the rest of his men. Viridius stood to face them, his sword resting lightly over his shoulder. As Aksutamoon closed in on him, a multicolored arrow flew from behind Viridius and thudded between the two men.

Viridius tilted his head to look at the arrow that was twice the length of a normal one. More arrows thudded next to it, and Aksutamoon's men came to a halt. With an arrow nocked, a figure came out of the woods, followed by others. The man with the raised longbow said nothing as he walked up. He was a full head taller than Viridius and built similarly.

"Do I know you?" Viridius asked, peering into the blackened hood.

One cold blue eye stared back at him. The man shouldered his bow, then punched Viridius in the stomach, doubling him over. An uppercut snapped Viridius's head back and knocked him unconscious. The figure rotated a gloved finger in the air and then dragged Viridius by one foot into the woods.

CHAPTER

Asinius woke up, bent over his saddle at the waist. His knuckles dragged against the ground, and his feet dangled on the opposite side.

"Gods dammit," he muttered, turning his head in several directions, looking for his riding companion. "Oi, anyone there?" Asinius asked.

All he could hear were the hoofbeats of his horse and another horse he couldn't see.

"I said, can anyone hear me?"

"I hear you," Tersius muttered.

The voice sounded familiar. He knew it wasn't the Wolfryian guards following him. If it were, he would already be in a shallow grave. He searched the landscape, attempting to get his bearings, but the dizziness from the blood rushing to his brain overwhelmed him. Asinius's pony came to a stop, and he heard Tersius dismount.

"I will give you whatever you desire if you free me from these bonds. I'll make you a very rich—"

Asinius's legs went over his head as Tersius threw his feet over the saddle. Tersius glanced at him and said, "No promises. My family is dead because you showed up at our doorstep." He kicked Asinius in the ribs. "Make ready. We are here," he said, yanking him to his feet.

Tersius pushed him down on a nearby rock. Asinius peered at the dust clouds behind them as riders descended the ridge. The unmistakable dark blue and white livery of Rebellium soldiers could clearly be seen as they rode toward them. No looking glass was needed.

The flag fluttering behind them was black with a broken bloody red and gold crown. Asinius closed his eyes and muttered a prayer as the men surrounded them, their spears leveled with Tersius's and Asinius's chests.

One of the men shouted down at them. "Not smart to come to these lands. Who are you, boy?"

"I am Tersius, son of Primus of West Drathia."

"Tersius?" the man asked, squinting.

"Aye, and I bring a traitor to the council."

The men on horseback inspected Asinius sitting on the rock. Using the flat of his spear blade, one of the men lifted his chin.

"Surprise," Asinius said with a wicked smile.

A few of the men grumbled under their breath, grabbed the hilt of their sword handles, and spat on him. Tersius threw them the rope he had tied around Asinius's wrists and walked in the direction the men had ridden from. The group leader yanked the rope and pulled Asinius closer to his men. He limped over to the group and stared at them defiantly.

One of the men pointed at Asinius. "Look at that, Calpernicus. He's got brass balls."

"Does he now?" Calpernicus said, hitting Asinius in the balls with the shaft of his spear.

Asinius fell to his knees, gasping in pain. Calpernicus's hazel eyes burned with hatred that had long simmered below the surface, just waiting to come out.

"Doesn't seem like it to me," Calpernicus said, dismounting near Asinius.

He walked up to him and pushed his forehead into his, forcing Asinius to turn away. "Oh, how I'm going to enjoy this traitor. You killed all our families in retribution for Tiberius. Now, I have no home, no wife—no life." Calpernicus shrugged and stared at his men's faces. "Well, no life worth living anyway. My wife, Valenia, was everything." Calpernicus's left hand clenched open and closed. "I promise you, Asinius, before today is done and the sun lowers behind us, I will carve you up like a chicken dinner."

Calpernicus pulled his knife and pinched Asinius's cheeks together. The knife slashed across Asinius's flesh from his ears to the corner of his mouth on both sides, giving him a permanent smile.

Asinius growled at him and spat out a torrent of blood. His growl should have been a cry for help, but Asinius wouldn't give them the satisfaction.

Calpernicus gave him a cold, distant smile and said, "My boys . . . ah, my beautiful boys." He blinked away a tear. "They knew what loyalty was, even when you cut them to pieces. They never muttered a word. Do you remember how old they were?"

"Can't say I even remember ordering their executions. Then again, boys should never follow the path of a traitor," Asinius mumbled, his cheeks splitting with each word.

With his forearms shaking, Calpernicus whispered, "You arrogant prick. Do you have any last words before we cut you to pieces and feed you to the dogs?"

Trying to keep his face from splitting, Asinius mumbled, "To hell with your families. I did them a favor, not letting them see what a terrible desolate and evil place Dellos has become."

Each of the men with Calpernicus sucked in their breath and dismounted. They circled him, sharpening their blades to begin their grim duty as grandfathers, fathers, and brothers. Many men in the Rebellium had to watch from a distance as their relatives were hung, drawn, and quartered, or beheaded for refusing to give them up. The spouses of the fighters suffered the most as they were slowly burned at the stake. Octavius thought he would receive their surrender and end the bloodshed. However, it had the opposite effect, and the war continued until there were too few fighters left in the Rebellium, and they melted into the shadows.

"By the Notella of the Drathian Code of Honor, I claim the traitor Asinius as my slave," shouted Tersius from behind them.

"Go to camp and find a whore, boy. Leave us to our dark business. It ends today," Calpernicus shouted over his shoulder.

"I said he's mine, by law."

Calpernicus put his hand on the man closest to Asinius and stopped him from cutting him.

"Do you know what you're doing, boy?" Calpernicus asked, barely able to control his emotions.

Tersius snatched the rope from Calpernicus's hand and said, "My father's dying command was to deliver him to the council to decide his fate. So that is where he will be taken."

The men stared at Tersius with frosty expressions but backed away. Invoking the right of Notella allowed for a slave or a prisoner of war not to be harmed. If the owner did not want to own the slave anymore, they would revoke their rights and give the individual a sword and shield in which to defend himself prior to setting them free.

Calpernicus crossed his arms over his chest and nodded. Tersius bowed at the waist and roughly put a burlap sack over Asinius's head. Asinius followed him blindly and fell a few times as they walked toward the camp. As they arrived at the walled gate, they were stopped by a sentry.

Tersius explained the situation, and the guard led them into the council's tent. Walking into the tent, Tersius saw a long, wooden table with ten chairs on one side of it. Four of the chairs had someone in them, and three of the chairs were leaning against the table, indicating that no one occupied them any longer. The last two were pushed in, waiting for their owners to return.

As Tersius entered, a man who had seen close to eighty summers was helped to his feet. He leaned on the top of his walking stick and squinted from behind his thick, round, wire-framed spectacles. After a few more moments of squinting, the old man turned a few feet to Tersius's left and said, "Primus?"

Sliding across the floor, Tersius stood in front of where he gazed and said, "No, Lord Valentinian, it is his youngest son," said a man standing beside Valentinian.

"Tersius. You should have said . . ." Valentinian paused and sniffed the air four times and closed his eyes. "You bring trouble and death to my camp, boy. You know better."

"I know, Lord Valentinian, but please, hear me out."

"All right, boy, where is your father? His seat waits for his return from the farm."

Tersius lowered his head, fighting back the warm tears that were rolling down his cheeks. A long silence followed as he finally blinked them away.

Valentinian nodded and quietly said, "Rest Primus's chair against the table. Cry not, boy. We will get revenge. Who do you bring to my tent?"

Tersius pulled the sack off Asinius's head. The members behind the table let out a hiss as they mumbled his name. Their old nemesis stood bleeding in front of them, but otherwise unrepentant. Valentinian sniffed the air, growled, and then waved for Tersius to push him forward. As Asinius neared the table, Valentinian swiftly struck him over the head with his cane and knocked him to the floor.

Bleeding in more than one spot, Asinius slowly regained his feet. Valentinian limped around the front of the table and swung his cane horizontally across Asinius's chest. He hit him twice more, once on each shoulder.

He glanced at Tersius with a smile. "Gods, that felt great. He may be your prisoner, boy, but if you want to replace your family at this table, you must execute this man in a fortnight."

"As you wish, m'lord. My father said the council should judge him. Where is Uncle Gius?"

"On an important mission. Stand the prisoner in the center of the room and light the fire," Valentinian said to the guard closest to him.

Valentinian raised his arms and said, "I, Lord Valentinian, Leader of the Free Armies of the Rebellium, hereby request the remaining members of the council to vote life or death for the prefect, Asinius Pelagius. He is charged with murder, torture, betrayal, and conduct unbecoming of a Wolfryian officer. How does the council vote?"

"Conduct unbecoming? The hell with you, Valentinian. I was an officer and a gentleman," Asinius mumbled, holding his cheeks.

The remaining members discussed his sentence quietly and then wrote down their decisions. Valentinian took the parchment and read the verdict. "Asinius Pelagius, Lead Centurion of Legion 1, it brings me great pleasure to tell you that you've been found guilty on all counts by the council and shall be punished according to the Old Laws. Do you have anything to say in your defense?" Valentinian asked.

Barely able to open his mouth, Asinius spat a stream of blood at Valentinian's sandaled feet, "Shit."

Tersius cut his eyes at Asinius while Valentinian laughed. "By the power given me by the Rebellium Council, I hereby sentence you to death. Your execution will take place in a fortnight from this evening." Pointing to a guard, Valentinian said, "Take him away."

Asinius held his head high, smiled at Tersius, and winked. He stopped next to him, swallowed a mouthful of blood, and whispered, "Careful where you walk, boy. There be monsters in this camp."

"Move along, " Tersius said, pushing Asinius toward the flap in the tent.

"Tersius, I am sorry about your father. I really am. He was a valuable leader and will be missed, but the loss of his command of the Free Armies will hurt us more," Valentinian said.

"Thank you, Lord Valentinian. I will follow the council's orders and execute Asinius in a fortnight and then go back to the farm," he said, turning to leave.

"I'm afraid I can't allow that," Valentinian said.

"And why the hell not?" Tersius asked, turning back around.

"Because we're the only family you have left. Your father gave explicit instructions should anything happen to him that we were to care for you. We were told to burn the farmhouse and keep you until you came of age. So you can either join us or—" he said with a shrug, looking around, "or join us. You really have no choice."

Tersius stared at the faces of the council. He pulled his sword from over his shoulder and slammed it into the ground. "I will leave when I want. You have no authority over me, m'lord. When Asinius has been executed, I will leave. If someone at this council chooses to challenge me, we will fight to the death," Tersius said, pulling his sword free from the dirt.

He turned his back to the council and walked out of the tent.

Valentinian grinned. "Just like your father."

CHAPTER

Corcundia leaned against the tree and studied the group of men sitting cross-legged around the fire ten feet away. She never heard them approach from behind, and it bothered her. Not one twig snapped under their weight during their approach. She thought for a moment and stared at them, trying to find out what kingdom they hailed from. A quick glance allowed her to see the soles of their shoes were covered with green leaves.

Aksutamoon and his men were bound like animals and hidden further away in the shadows. Sniffing the air, Corcundia thought she smelled a wet dog. One of the men stood up and walked over to them. A single blue eye stared at her from under a black head wrap. She waited for the stranger to speak first so she could gain an advantage in knowing where they came from. With a slight purr, the stranger knelt in front of her and said, "Where do you come from?"

EMPERORS & ASSASSINS | 131

"Could you say that again?"

With a sigh, the voice purred again, "Where do you come from? North or South?"

"Lady Corcundia of Vitadruma is my name. I am from East Drathia, and we are headed for the Rebellium's headquarters."

Unwinding his head wrap, the stranger revealed the head of a lion. Corcundia gasped and pulled back. She crossed her fingers in front of her face. "Shit, you are real."

The being sat down and licked his paws. He rubbed his ears and said, "Pardon my look. I didn't mean to scare you."

"How do you speak . . .?" she asked.

Holding up his furry paw, he said, "Our slaves."

"You're slavers?"

The lion humanoid bowed his head, never taking his pale blue eye from her, and said, "Guilty." He smiled, revealing his razor-sharp incisors.

Closing his fist over his heart, the lion man said, "My name's K'aro, of the mighty D'atu. We were on our way back from a hunting—"

"You mean a slave run," she said, slicing his sentence off.

He snarled but regained his composure. "Yes, a slave run. We live by selling flesh. You wouldn't understand, human. And, yes, our main source of coin is from selling your kind. I think there is more money in precious metals and stones in the Lava Lands, but our leader, Dro'ka, decides where we go," K'aro growled.

"So, you follow him like he's your master. Is he your master, dog?"

Baring his incisors, K'aro growled again and then touched his muzzle to her nose. "See to your companions. We leave in a few hours." He stood up and then turned around. "I almost forgot." He pulled an apple from his pocket. "Make sure you get your strength up. You'll need it," he said, rewrapping the cloth around his head.

The sun rose the next morning, but gray and white clouds hid it. Corcundia, Gius, and Viridius walked a few paces in front of her remaining men. Aksutamoon and his men were loaded into caged wagons further back. One of Corcundia's men collapsed next to her, and she knelt to help him. She heard a roar above her. Looking up, she saw a boot swing in her direction, but it was deflected at the last moment. She rolled aside and heard a barking voice.

"Leave her, Dro'ka. She is only trying to help her companion."

"You dare touch me, K'aro?"

Softly purring, K'aro said, "I claim this human as my slave. If I must, I will fight you for her."

Dro'ka stared at K'aro for a moment, baring his incisors. "Good," he roared.

The two warriors began circling each other as the other Ba in the group roared around them and slammed their swords into the earth. The sword ring they were forming was a traditional way for two warriors in the Ba culture to end their differences. Blood had to be taken if a challenge was issued, and if the insulted party won, they could kill the offender or make them a slave for the remainder of their days.

Dro'ka and K'aro freed their backup daggers and crossed them in front of their faces. The beginning ritual of the sword ring was a poetic dance between two combatants. The two warriors would circle each other and exchange salutes. Their fellow warriors would hum a melodic tune as the warriors wove their knives intricately around their bodies.

The next phase saw both warriors kneeling in the center of the ring. They shoved their daggers into the ground up to the hilt in front of them. One combatant stuck his left paw out, and the other stuck his right paw out. A rope was tied around each warrior's wrist, and after a count to five, the pair stood and commenced the attack.

K'aro knew he could not beat Dro'ka. He simply stayed in a kneeling position when the contest began.

"Off your knees, coward," Dro'ka roared.

K'aro began to hum the same melody as his shield brothers, as he glanced around the ring with his one eye. Dro'ka yanked him to the center.

Holding a knife to his throat, Dro'ka shouted, "Fight or die."

"Give me death," K'aro said, lifting his chin.

Shaking his head, Dro'ka roared and walked away. "Damn you, K'aro. You're my only healer. You are now my prisoner and will answer to me. Take him and put him in with the other slaves."

As he was led away, K'aro made eye contact with Lady Corcundia. He lifted his head and smiled, his incisors glinting in the sun. Dro'ka led through fear and intimidation and killed any and all who opposed him.

Standing nearly nine feet in height, he had silver fur with black spots running along his arms and a crescent moon branded on each of his forearms. He looked old, exactly how old, Corcundia could only guess.

As the group traveled, the tall tips of volcanoes could be seen in the distance as they crossed further into the Lava Lands.

Viridius glanced at Corcundia and nodded his head toward the volcanoes and muttered, "The ancestral home of the Ba. We won't live long now."

"Can we escape?" she asked.

"Nah, they know every trail. We would be dead before we made it a hundred feet," Viridius explained.

A whip cracked near Viridius's head, and they stopped speaking. The group trudged through the thick ash, the air around them heavy with heat. The further they walked, the more they sweat, and the dryer their mouths became. Viridius was the first to see a cluster of tents in a large circle over the next ridge, and a smaller encampment could be seen near the mouth of the river a few hundred yards upstream. As the entourage came over the last dune, they saw a bridge that crossed a river of lava.

Several warriors dressed in golden armor guarded the bridge to the main encampment. They stood nine feet in height, similar to Dro'ka. Their fur was jet black, and their eyes bright yellow. They crossed their weapons at the entrance as the group approached, blocking the bridge.

Dro'ka dismounted and placed his clenched fist over his heart. "I am Dro'ka, leader of the Runners."

The guards didn't move or speak to him. Growling under his breath at their insolence, he roared, "I am Dro'ka, leader of the Runners. I command you to move aside!"

The guards chuckled and stared at him. The power he once held was gone among the Protectors. K'aro approached from behind and nodded. The guards nodded back at him and stood at parade rest. With a roar, the guards slammed the butts of their spears into the ground and spun to the side.

Dro'ka bared his incisors at K'aro and continued into the encampment. The humans were led to a caged area surrounded by wooden spikes spread out every six inches. Dro'ka shoved Viridius, Aksutamoon, and their men in, but yanked Corcundia's rope as she followed the others, knocking her to the ground.

She knelt and tried to get up before Dro'ka stomped her into the dirt. Viridius pulled with all his strength and tried to break the bars of the cage. His muscles rippled, and sweat dripped from his brow.

"You furry bastard, try that on me!" he shouted.

Dro'ka glared at him and then dragged Corcundia's body away, leaving a trail in the dry dirt. Viridius stood seething at the door of the enclosure.

"Well, she's dead," Gius said with a sigh of resignation. "Damn shame. We needed her too."

Allies were hard to come by in Dellos, especially for him. Running from the Wolfryian Empire through the last year had caused Gius more heartache than he wanted. His family was dead, and not a single soul outside of the Rebellium camp knew he existed. He knew Octavius would hunt every member down until they were all swinging from the end of a rope, so he tried to stay as low key as possible.

"You don't give a shit about anyone, Viridius. Why the theatrics?" Gius asked.

"You're right. I don't. I only care about that horse over there," he said, staring across the camp at the stable where their confiscated horses were being kept. "But Corcundia owes me money for services rendered. Unless you want to pay that too?" Viridius asked, cutting his eyes at Gius.

If there was one thing Viridius liked about his captors, it was their care of animals. He made mental notes about the strengths and weaknesses of the camp as he looked around. Escape wasn't a feasible option as he counted the Ba at different locations around the camp. Slavery didn't look promising either as he saw human heads rotting on spikes spaced evenly around the campsite.

"There is no escape, only death," said a gravelly voice under a hood near them on the outside of the enclosure.

Viridius turned at the sound and shook his head. "Watch who you sneak up on, cur," he muttered.

A slight chuckle escaped from under the hood. The hunchback figure moved closer to the gate, his knuckles dragging in the sand.

Viridius wrinkled his nose and leaned backward. Gagging, he drew his head back as far as he could. "You smell like death."

"Not yet, but I will get there eventually," said the voice.

Viridius and Gius took a step forward, inspecting the figure.

"Boo!" the man said with a cackle, pulling back his hood.

Viridius tripped over Gius as they backed up, startled by the man's features. The man's forehead was the length of two hands stacked on one another. He had a hole for one ear, and the other looked like cauliflower.

"What are you?" Viridius gasped, crossing his fingers in front of his face to ward off evil spirits.

"That's funny. I'm a human, like you. Discarded by my parents in the woods north of here as a baby. The Ba found me on a hunting expedition and brought me to the Lava Lands. They named me Nigol," he said, showing them two daggers and the key."And I'll give you these if you take me with you."

"Whaddya want in return?" Viridius asked.

"Find me a woman to settle down with. I want a family before I die," Nigol said.

"Why not find a whore?" Viridius asked, pinching his nose, trying not to stare at him.

Nigol's eyes softened, and he stared at his feet. "Because what you see on the outside can give life to something beautiful inside and out," he whispered.

"Great, a cripple with a heart of gold. I've heard of a whore with a heart of gold, but this is too much," Viridius said, grasping the hilt of one of the daggers in Nigol's hands.

"Do I have your word?" Nigol asked, holding up the key for them to see.

"Aye, you have our word. When we have our other companion, we will depart. Now why don't you make yourself useful and tell us some things about this camp and our host," Viridius said, taking a knee in the dirt.

Nigol smiled, his missing front teeth poking through.

"The group that brought you in are known as Runners. Slave hunters who go to the worst parts of Dellos and bring back the best humans to trade in. The only member of their group who's not terrible is K'aro. He's their healer, and if he could escape with us, he would be useful."

Viridius nodded and then pointed at the Ba wearing different types of armor. Nigol continued, "The ones wearing golden armor are known as Protectors. They are camp guards and live a life of solitude. No mate, no cubs. Death in battle is their only goal. It is the only group a warrior can be disowned from." Nigol smiled before he continued. "The one walking over there is Dro'ka. He has the mark of the disowned," he whispered.

Viridius's ears perked up when he mentioned Dro'ka. Nigol continued, "Most of the disowned become part of The Outkast Clan, a group of outlaws sent to live by Lava Lake as punishment. They wait patiently for redemption, a redemption that may never come. Dro'ka was banished from the Protectors as well, but he's a great slave hunter, so the elders took him back."

Viridius pointed at a warrior as he walked by.

Nigol continued his story. "The ones in blue armor are Seekers. They keep the history of the Ba in their books and drawings. The everyday warriors you see wear plain green armor. They make up most of the pride's warriors and do the bulk of the fighting during war. Their lionesses and cubs are never close to any humans. They believe we carry diseases they can become afflicted with. Lastly, you have human slaves. Men, women, and children plucked from

Dellos to do whatever the Ba require. We obviously matter little," he said, finishing his rundown as he looked at a head impaled on a spike.

"Dro'ka. Tell me of him," Viridius said.

"What's there to say? He loves causing others pain. One day when he least expects it, someone is going to jam a knife in his spine."

"Who . . . you?" Viridius asked with a chuckle.

"No, sir. I am no great warrior, but he did the unthinkable when he killed my master. He murdered his brother and father and took control of their pride, the D'atu. In their society, there is no greater evil than killing their kin."

Glad I ain't one of these things. Viridius spat on the ground at his feet and thought of his brother and father's blood on his hands, still haunting his nightmares.

Father and Palix would still be alive had they not joined that assassination attempt.

"Which reminds me. The plan we talked about before our mishaps," Gius said, interrupting them.

Viridius cut his eyes in Gius's direction. *We are about to get eaten, and he still wants to save Dellos.*

Eyebrow raised, Viridius asked him, "What did you have in mind?"

"Let's get to my camp. It's not far," Gius said.

Viridius nodded and then turned his head to Nigol and said, "I need you to steal that black horse over there and have fresh horses for the others. Find out where they are keeping our companion, Corcundia. Then find all our weapons and armor and bring them to us."

"And I'm coming with you?"

"Get me what I asked for, and, yes, we'll take you," Viridius hissed.

"It will be done," Nigol said, disappearing into the night.

CHAPTER

Twelve

"Mercy, m'lord, mercy!" screamed the man being tortured by Octavius.

The cat-o'-nine-tails ripped flesh from the man's back as Octavius swung it again. He grinned as he continued to whip the man until he passed out. The other four men hadn't fared any better in the dungeon. They were all nailed by both their hands and feet across two wooden planks.

The dungeon was poorly illuminated with rats and other vermin chasing their heels. A few torches lined the walls as stagnant water fell from the ceiling and onto the bodies. Drops of water could be heard as they landed in the puddles of blood and water mixed together on the floor. Primus's dead body lay beside Marus.

"Marus, did I not tell these men to return with Asinius?" Octavius asked.

The hair on Marus's neck stood on edge. He took a step back and nodded silently.

"Then why do I have a dead body? Not that I'm unhappy with the results. Primus was on my list anyway, so killing them was perfect. I still can't believe they hid so close." He paused in thought. "However, your men—"

"Imperator, those were not my men, they—"

Octavius moved faster than Marus would have thought. He slammed a dagger against Marus's throat. "They . . . are . . . your . . . men . . . because I say they are. I'm emperor, and that means they can be anything I want them to be."

Marus lowered his eyes and looked away.

"Tell me, Prefect, why do I not have Asinius or Viridius?"

Marus stared straight-ahead. "They elude us, Imperator. We are trying to locate them as we speak."

Octavius turned and walked over to the table where his torture tools were and grabbed another cat-o'-nine. He spun and slammed the whip over Marus's head, stunning him. His second blow came down before Marus could recover.

Marus threw his arms up to block the blows and then stepped back ever so slightly. As he retreated, he tripped and fell to the floor. Octavius whipped him across the back until thick, red blood soaked the back of his tunic.

"You." Octavius pointed to one of his guards. "Kick him until you hear something break, or he dies."

The man bowed and kicked Marus until he heard a sickening crunch. Marus groaned as he felt two of his ribs break. Octavius squatted on his haunches and yanked Marus's bloody head up.

"I am Octavius Victorus, the one true ruler of Dellos. Remember who runs Wolfryia and the worthless people in it. I want to hear one thing from you right now," he whispered, slamming Marus's face into a bloody puddle.

"As you say . . ." Marus gasped as his head came out of the water. "So shall it be."

"Don't forget who owns you, Marus," Octavius said, oblivious to the fact that Marus's blood was seeping onto his fresh toga.

A little freckled cherublike giddy boy ran down the steps behind them and yelled, "Uncle Octavius, Uncle Octavius!"

"Ah, Zactus," Octavius responded with open arms and an energetic smile. He snatched his nephew into a bear hug. "What are you doing down here?"

Zactus laughed. "You were supposed to take me on a grand adventure today, silly."

Laughing, Octavius said, "Was I . . . oh yes, now I remember. Shall we go?" he asked, rubbing the boy's thick, black hair.

Octavius stopped at Marus's head, and without looking down, he hissed, "Either Asinius and Viridius are found in a fortnight, or you take their place on the chopping block. It matters little to me. Any head will do. I love my nephew, and I don't want him to see you tortured. He saved your life today, Marus. You should thank him."

Marus glanced at the boy. "Thank you, Prince Zactus."

"Good dog. Now, where were we, Zactus?" Octavius asked.

Cackling loudly, Zactus yelled, "An adventure."

"Ah yes, an adventure," Octavius said, walking Zactus to the door, his guards following him out.

The next morning, Marus rolled onto his side as he lay on the freezing dungeon floor. He looked at his men in their tortured positions and then crawled over to them. Four of the men had died overnight, impaled on the boards. The room smelled of shit from the men's bowels evacuating. Their bodies were cold, frozen like stone. Marus pulled himself up, checked their pulses at the base of their necks, and made sure they had expired. Only one man barely hung to life.

Marus stared at him. "You're still alive?"

"I'm still alive," the man said, making a feeble attempt at raising his head.

"You should be dead from that cat-o'-nine beating."

"Lucky for you, I'm tough to kill," the older legionnaire mumbled.

"Where is Asinius?" Marus demanded, his breath hot against the man's cheek.

"I thought you told us to go out there and kill whoever harbored him. We tracked him to the farm, and he escaped. You told me not to kill him, Marus . . . for old times' sake. Don't you remember?" the old man said.

"Things have changed. It's all about self-preservation now, and it starts with my preservation. He won't get a pass now but thank you for your hard work, cousin. I'll take it from here," Marus said, thrusting his dagger into his cousin's throat.

"Why—" mouthed his cousin, the blood draining from his face.

Marus smirked with a shrug as he wiped his blade clean and said, "Why? Why the hell not?"

Marus limped over to the other men and cut their throats to ensure they were dead. Then he moved to the dungeon door and went back to his quarters.

His slave, Laticius, was boiling water for his bath as he entered. Seeing Marus, he moved to his side and helped him to bed.

"M'lord, are you OK?"

Marus nodded and pointed to the wine carafe on a nearby table filled with Tramonian Tears. Laticius bowed and brought him a cup filled to the brim.

Marus smacked his lips together. "That's the good stuff." He took a deep breath. "Ready my pack and gear. We leave in the morning."

Asinius's fingers wrapped around the slate-colored bars of his cell, the wounds on his cheeks bothering him to no end. He counted seven days since the first sunset, a constant reminder of impending execution. The only thing left in his cell was a bucket to shit in and some straw to lie on.

A drunken surgeon had come to see him on the first night and cauterized his cheeks with a thin poker. The skin on his face had itched uncontrollably afterward, causing him to pat it so he wouldn't rip the wounds open again. The gray hair follicles growing in on his beard seemed to pulsate painfully as the days wore on. His captors fed him porridge and cups of water, barely enough to keep him alive.

Calpernicus, the man who had cut his cheeks, walked by and stopped in front of the cell with his men. Holding a mug of ale in his hand, he hiccuped and stared at Asinius for a moment. "I'm glad you like horse oats."

"Horse oats?" Asinius asked with his mouth full.

Calpernicus laughed. "You're eating the mill left from our horses. You think we would feed our most hated prisoner any of *our* precious food?"

Asinius spat the porridge out of his mouth and mumbled, "You better hope they kill me, 'cause if they don't, I'll repay you for what you have done to me," he said, refusing to break his gaze.

One of Calpernicus's men walked up and jabbed Asinius in the side with the shaft of his spear. Asinius fell to his knees, wheezing and coughing. Roaring with laughter, Calpernicus spat on him while he was bent over.

"You're no better than a slave, Asinius. You never were a great leader, we—"

"Calpernicus, that's enough!" Tersius shouted, coming out of the shadows. "You know he belongs to me. I won't say it again."

Calpernicus turned his head and said, "Watch your mouth, boy, or I'll eat your liver."

Tersius rubbed his clammy hands across his pant legs and advanced. Six against one were not good odds, but there was no way to back down. Standing in front of the men, he placed his hand on his sword hilt and waited, shifting his weight from one leg to the other.

Calpernicus's lip sneered upward, and he said, "You got your father's heart, boy." He glanced over his shoulder at Asinius and said, "Lucky for you the kid showed up when he did. Real lucky. But don't fret; your luck will run out."

Without another word, Calpernicus and his men walked away. Tersius approached within a few feet of the cage and produced some lettuce he had found. Asinius tried to look disinterested in the food, but his growling stomach gave it away. Tersius handed it to him and then sat down in front of the cell.

"Asinius, you're going to tell me how you knew my father and why he was ready to kill you when you last met."

A piece of lettuce stuck out of Asinius's mouth as he nibbled it like a rabbit. With a deep groan, he pressed his back against the bars. He pursed his lips together and forcefully exhaled with a wince. Not sure how to begin, he stared into the clouds as the rays of sun tried to burst through. "All right, I'll tell you. But you have to make sure I get more food. I will not die on an empty stomach."

"Deal," Tersius said.

"So, you want to know what happened before you were born, eh?" Asinius asked.

"I want to know something in particular."

Asinius raised an eyebrow.

"My father said Wolfryians ordered my mother killed. Is that true?" Tersius asked, staring through him.

Asinius's cherublike demeanor changed. "That's irrelevant. Octavius wanted everything and everyone who was part of the Rebellium killed. If they knew, or he thought they knew . . . they died. He ensured they suffered terribly, knowing their families watched from a distance. Spiked heads lined the road to the crossroads in central Dellos."

"And I care? I'll ask you again. Who stuck their sword in my mother's stomach?"

Asinius cast his eyes down to the dirt and shook his head. "The soldier—"

"Executioner. A soldier doesn't kill innocents, old man," Tersius shouted over him.

Asinius raised his eyes and said, "Wake up, boy. There are no innocents: only the quick or the dead. And as for who killed your mother, it doesn't matter. She's dead. Move on."

"You know, don't you?" Tersius asked, acrimoniously.

A thin smile crossed Asinius's lips. "Oh aye," he said, walking to the other side of the cage.

Tersius ran to the other side with him and said, "Tell me who it was, slave, and I will try to spare your life."

"There will come a day when you know, but it won't be from me. You want to spare my life, that's your choice," Asinius said.

Tersius bristled. "Fine. But this conversation isn't over. I can make sure you get a key, but you have to give me some information about Iceport first."

"What do you want to know?" Asinius asked, licking his lips.

"How many troops does the emperor have?"

"Three legions, totaling three thousand men, but only two are in fighting shape. The other is for show."

"How many men guard the emperor at night?"

Asinius raised an eyebrow and sighed. "Boy, you ask questions that you have no business knowing. You should let Valentinian come and ask me." Smelling the air around him, Asinius said, "You reek of lies. I know your father taught you not to lie. So don't."

Feigning surprise, Tersius shrugged and said, "Valentinian doesn't know I'm here. So, tell me, and I'll bring you more food than you have eaten in weeks."

"Don't attempt to bribe me. It's beneath you. Octavius wants me dead, obviously, and it's why I'm here with you. If I wasn't on his kill list, do you think I would be locked in this cage?" he asked, shaking the bars vigorously.

"Quiet down, old man, before the guard comes back."

Just as Tersius said it, a guard walked by them, staring at Asinius, who rested his forearms against the bars. Asinius lifted his head, flipped the guard the bird, and then tried to spit on him. The guard dodged it and quickly smashed the end of his spear over Asinius's knuckles.

"You son of—"

"Say something about me mother, and I'll kill you," the guard said menacingly before returning to his patrol.

Asinius watched the man walk away, his eyes boring holes in his back. "You were saying bo—?" He looked around.

No one was there.

CHAPTER

Fire pits blazed around the Ba camp as the sun set. The purple sunsets over the Lava Lands were always a good omen, but they only happened a few times a year, and tonight marked the new year. Viridius sat with his back against the bars, staring at Aksutamoon across the cage.

All you need to do is fall asleep, and I'm going to slice your throat, Viridius thought.

Aksutamoon had no intention of dying with his eyes closed, throat exposed. Trakuta stared at Viridius, touched his broken nose, and winced. It had been a long time since someone had gotten the drop on him, and he was waiting patiently for revenge.

"When he turns his back to you, kill him," Aksutamoon said, staring straight ahead.

Trakuta nodded and walked over to Viridius.

"Mind if I sit?" he asked.

"I don't own the dirt," Viridius mumbled.

As Trakuta sat down, Viridius asked him, "How's the beak?"

"Broken, thanks for that. I—"

"I know you're going to try to kill me. You and the fat ape over there whisper like whores in a confessional booth," Viridius said.

"I don't know what you're talking about. I just came to get a better lay of the land for our escape," Trakuta said with a shrug.

Viridius laughed. "Glad you're an assassin and not a politician in Wolfryia. You lie like a boy trying to fuck a tavern wench. Now, either you can help us escape, and we can travel together out of here, or . . ." Viridius paused and pulled the blade Nigol had given him from his cloak, "you'll get enough time for a prayer."

Trakuta smiled, showing his unusually pearly white teeth. His tattoos glowed in the moonlight, his eyes an unnatural light blue.

"What do you suggest?" Trakuta asked.

Viridius shrugged. "What's with the tattoos, by the way?"

Trakuta chuckled. "A line for every man I've killed. They were put on by a shaman in my tribe and glow in the moonlight."

Viridius glanced over his shoulder. "Nice story. To answer your earlier question, I was looking around, and I found our best escape route lies through the ravine. But with lava and ash on both sides, it's going to make it tough to outrun those big bastards. For a true escape, we will need some of the men to fight a rearguard action." Thinking for a moment, Viridius continued. "We have your thirty and a few of Lady Corcundia's. All told, around forty men. We have to find Corcundia, rescue her, and then try to reach the ravine before these things know what hit them."

Trakuta bared his open palms and said, "We have no weapons. If we try, we can only hold them for a few seconds."

"That's why I need your help. I'll get our weapons and armor. You get me four fools who will die because you asked them too," Viridius said, watching Nigol cross from one tent to another.

"I'm only a spoke on the wheel," Trakuta said with a smile.

"Then convince your *king* to order their deaths. Doesn't matter to me."

"I'll see what I can do," Trakuta said, heading to the other side of the cage.

Viridius turned back around and watched Nigol make several trips back to the cage. He tracked down all their weapons and armor during the festivities and hauled them back to the enclosure.

Aksutamoon approached from the other side of the cage and said, "Trakuta has talked to me. What's the plan?"

"I'll save your miserable hides, but it's going to cost you fifty thousand gold coins," Viridius said, straightening his chain mail.

Not moving an inch, Aksutamoon glared at him. "How can I trust you won't turn on me?"

"You can't. Now, do we have an accord?" Viridius asked.

"Fifty thousand? All right, fifty thousand it is. But if you betray me, I'll take my time cutting pieces off of you, starting with your feet."

Viridius smiled and looked at Nigol. "Where is Lady Corcundia?" he asked.

"She's in the tent with the other slave women."

"Other slave women? Are there other slaves?" Gius asked, butting into the conversation.

"Hey, Gius, stop trying to save the world for a day and let us ride outta here without a wagon train of flesh these creatures sell to feed their young. Be glad it ain't you. Think, man. We don't have the manpower to fight them. They will catch us, cook us, and then eat us," Viridius said.

"Absolutely under no circumstance will I leave these people behind," Gius said.

Exasperated, Viridius replied, "Why is everything so black and white with you, Gius? Come over to the gray side for a bit. It won't kill you. I might, but it won't. It will be a refreshing way to see it from a different angle."

Gius shot him a cold stare and didn't respond.

I know I hit a nerve.

"Maybe it will kill you if I'm lucky enough. All I know is that I don't care about these people," Viridius said.

"I could care less if you agree with me, Viridius. We save these people, and then we go to my camp. Do you want to get paid?" Gius asked, crossing his arms over his chest.

Throwing his hands up, Viridius said, "Gods dammit."

Nigol walked up and looked over his shoulder, trying to quiet everyone down. A guard came out of a tent nearby and looked over at the cages.

"Please, be quiet. The guard—"

"If you slaves talk anymore, I'll kill one of you for every word you mutter," the guard growled in broken Dellosian, then ducked back into his tent.

Reemerging from the shadows, Nigol continued, "As I was saying, please don't fight. Slaves are sacrificed on nights like this for the perfect sunsets. They don't need a reason to please their gods. They enjoy killing us."

Aksutamoon looked over at him and said, "Leave, slave. This doesn't involve you."

Nigol's head dropped as he began to shuffle back into the shadows.

Viridius's fist clenched by his side. "Talk to him like that again, and I'll cut your royal head off ya lardship. King or no king, I'll kill you all the same. Unlike you, *he* has a way to get us out of here. He holds more value than you do, so shut your rich lips, or I'll glue them shut," he said, ensuring Aksutamoon saw the blade in his palm.

Nigol looked at Viridius, as did Gius, both shocked he would stick up for him. Nigol was hardly seen, but always listening and knew every path in the Lava Lands.

Viridius glanced up at him as he peered at them from outside the cage. "All right, Nigol, which tent is Corcundia in, and how many are guarding her?" he asked.

"I don't know how many guard her, but she's in the center of the camp where Dro'ka sleeps with the Runners," he said.

"Forget the others; we get her and leave. Any man who wants to stay and help them can, but those who want to live will follow me. So, let's decide who's going to go, and who's going to stay," Viridius said.

Corcundia's men quickly joined Viridius while Gius stood by himself. Aksutamoon and his men stood with their backs against the bars. Viridius scanned their half-hidden features in the darkness. "Aksutamoon, are you with Gius or me?"

"Neither. I would rather kill both of you." He walked over to where Gius stood with his arms crossed and said, "However, I ask you not to sacrifice your life for no reason, Gius. Please come to Tramonia as my guest, and I will help you take Iceport. And then we can help you save these people in the Lava Lands."

Gius smiled at Viridius about his newfound fortune and stepped forward to answer Aksutamoon. "I will follow you—"

Aksutamoon punched Gius, and Viridius could hear the sound several feet away.

"That should shut up the voice of insanity. Can't save everybody," Aksutamoon whispered.

Viridius chuckled and shook his head. He glanced back at Nigol. "That solves one problem, Nigol. How many men can we safely get over to Corcundia's tent?"

"You, me, and three others. There are two guards by the closest fire, another two nearby, and Dro'ka's floating around here somewhere," Nigol said, glancing over his shoulder in fear.

"Let's get a plan together and get out of here," Viridius said, binding Gius by his hands and feet.

Asinius covered himself as the rain fell into his cell. It was nice to have an open cell during the days with nice weather, but when it rained, or the wind blew hard, it was murderous. He had weaved almost all the hay in the cell for his bedding, and the leftovers were used to make a thatch that hung above him.

Dellosian rain was warm to the touch, like the mist of a waterfall, which was more of a hindrance than anything else. Asinius pissed in the corner as the thunder roared through the night sky. The longer he was held captive, the more he got used to the noise. A pair of boots silently walked up to the cage behind him and waited for another clap of thunder.

"Get up earlier than that, boy," Asinius said, buttoning his pants.

"How did you know?" Tersius asked, moving out of the shadow.

"I heard you before you opened my cell door. Try again tomorrow. Now, are you here to talk again?" Asinius asked.

"Yes, I want to know more."

"Keep digging in shit, boy, and you may not be able ever to clean your hands," Asinius scolded him.

"Don't treat me like a child. I'm seventeen summers," Tersius said.

Asinius laughed. "Oh, are you now? My apologies, I guess you're all grown up."

"I must be because they gave me the order to execute you."

Asinius paused as he weaved the remaining hay into a hole in the thatched roof. "Is that a fact? They're sending a boy to do a man's job now? Lord Valentinian must be getting desperate. Some of the chairs in his tent were leaning forward. Do you know why they are like that?"

"Yeah, you killed the owners," Tersius muttered.

"Is that what you think? Oh, I'm a bastard, all right, but not an executioner. It is true I tracked and captured the Rebellium scum when they fled throughout Dellos, but I didn't chop anyone's head off myself. I ordered it done. That's a different animal altogether. Now, where is my extra food you promised?" Asinius asked.

Tersius shoved the sack into Asinius's arms, then pressed him for answers. "Is that how you sleep at night? I always thought ordering and executing were the same thing. My father told me you killed everyone. You think there is a difference?" he asked.

"Boy, don't question my ethics or morals, for that matter. I've killed men for less, and while I like you, I would have no problem running my blade through your guts. I made my decision, and I know the costs. You know nothing of sacrifice," Asinius said, his voice even.

"You're right. My father knew sacrifice, while I, on the other hand, know the cost. I'll tell you what I do know. Ethics are the code of right or wrong, like my belief in Notella, which saved your life, by the way. And morals are about what a man personally believes when faced with difficult decisions. I may be young, but I ask you to remember who I was raised by."

Asinius pressed his tongue against his teeth, clucked, and said, "So, boy, you believe you know what life is? I'll show you what loyalty gets you."

He pulled his tunic up and showed Tersius his battle scars. "The line across my stomach is from an ax in my first battle. Nearly killed me. The stab wounds," he said, pointing over his heart, "happens when a woman is scorned. And now this," he said, touching his cheeks.

Tersius stared at his scars for a moment and noticed the deep purple color from his hip bone just below his waist. Asinius caught his stare. "And this one almost cost me my life. A fight I neither wanted nor cared about," Asinius said, pulling his breeches down, revealing a long, jagged scar that ran down his leg on the front and back.

"What—"

"This is the cost of fighting for an insane emperor. I stepped in front of a blow meant for him and nearly lost my leg. And what happened to me in the end? Tiberius's dirty bastard son tried to kill me."

"My father was right. None of you get it," Tersius said.

"Get what?" Asinius asked, pulling his tunic back down.

"The Wolfryian emperors want sheep, mindless sheep he used to say. And now, you're in a cage, and it fits you," Tersius said, bleating like a sheep as he shook the bars.

Asinius pushed his face into the bars and shouted, "You ever make that sound again, and I will kill you. I would rather die than betray Wolfryia. My honor will not be questioned, especially not by a snot-nosed little brat."

Tersius paused, rested his head against the bars, and whispered, "You said you knew who killed my mother."

"Ach, yes, but—"

Tersius raised his eyes and said, "Speak, or I'll kill you before I parade you to the chopping block."

Asinius lifted his neck and said, "You're a cherry if you do."

Tersius planted his feet and kept his fingers on the hilt of his knife, but didn't move.

"Bah, you're gutless, boy—gutless," Asinius said, turning his back to him.

Tersius fumbled with the key and yanked the door to his cell open and said, "Gutless?"

Asinius turned, disarmed him, and then kicked the inside of his thigh, crumpling him to the ground.

"Your anger betrays your footsteps. I am not your enemy, boy. But I will leave you with this."

Asinius drew his fist back, brought it down on Tersius's chin, and knocked him unconscious. He laid him down and rummaged through his waistband. Asinius took his coin purse and knife and then sprinted for the door. As he reached the door, it slammed shut on his fingers.

"Fuck," he shouted, holding his bent fingers, blowing on them with pursed lips.

Asinius glanced up and saw Calpernicus wearing a light smile on his face. "Not so fast, you murderin' bastard. I'll see your head removed from your shoulders before I die. Now bring the boy over here."

Asinius grabbed Tersius's hands and dragged him to the door.

"Now, back up, slave," Calpernicus demanded.

Asinius held his hands up and walked to the back of the cage. Calpernicus looked at the men with him and waved them in.

"Hands where I can see them, old man. Hands where I can see them."

Tersius woke the following morning with a loud groan, holding his jaw. "What the—"

"Easy, boy. Asinius knocked you out. My men stopped him from cutting your throat when he attacked you," Calpernicus said, handing him a drinking horn.

Hesitating, Tersius took a long swig, spat it up, and coughed violently. Calpernicus laughed and pushed the horn to his lips again.

"A man drinks, he kills, and dies for the cause. Are you one of us?" Calpernicus asked, his right eyebrow raised.

"Don't know," Tersius said, trying to repress his gag reflex on his next swig. He wiped the back of his hand across his lips, trying to remove the sting.

"Either you are, or you aren't. It would be a damn shame for someone from such an illustrious family as yours not to follow in his father's footsteps."

"And what footsteps are those?" Tersius asked.

"Free from the yoke of the empire," Calpernicus said.

Tersius shrugged. "I don't understand."

"Do you believe all of us should bow to the crown?"

Staring at his feet, Tersius shook his head and tried to change the subject. "How do you know Asinius?"

Smiling, Calpernicus pulled a plug of tobacco from his pocket and offered him some. Tersius declined.

Calpernicus rubbed his palms around his mouth with a sigh. "I know that piece of shit from my days as an infantry commander in the Wolfryian army. I rebelled with your uncle Gius and your father. And now, we are all that remain of the original rebels." Calpernicus pointed at his men. "They were all friends of your father's at one time or another, and all of them, without exception, saw their families slaughtered. Your father at least managed to capture Asinius, and that will allow us our revenge. Might even make something positive out of a shitty situation."

"You won't kill Asinius, Calpernicus. He is my slave, so he's mine to kill. I'll kill anyone that goes near him," Tersius said.

Calpernicus growled. "Look, boy, I've spent most of my life serving people like him in Wolfryia. I've been waiting for the day I could cut his guts out and roast 'em over a fire. I wanted him alive so he could watch his own death." He paused for a moment and chuckled. "It's by luck you even knew to claim the old code of Notella, and it doesn't really have a place in modern society. But Valentinian believes in it, and as long as he runs our outfit, we have no other choice but to allow it. But if you turn your back for one second, I'll kill that son of a whore."

Tersius bristled, but let the comment rest. He switched topics. "So, what was your reason for rebelling?" he asked, passing the wine back to him.

Calpernicus smirked. "I joined because I believe every Wolfryian citizen loyal to the crown should be tortured, then burned. If they are not peasantish in nature, they shouldn't be in power."

"Peasantish?"

"Yea, hard workers like my men." Pausing, he glanced at Tersius. "And dare I say, you."

"You don't even know me," Tersius said.

"I knew your family, and that's all I need to know," he replied.

"And why did my family join?" Tersius asked.

"Everyone has their own reason. They never told me."

Tersius exhaled. "That figures."

Calpernicus spat a stream of tobacco juice from between his lips. He muttered, "We all have choices, don't we?"

Tersius made eye contact with Calpernicus. "What's so special about the cause?" Tersius inquired.

"Everything. If we could manage to wipe out the blue bloods—"

Tersius interrupted him. "Blue bloods?"

Calpernicus smiled. "The aristocracy doesn't belong in power because they abuse it," he said.

"You really hate them that much?" Tersius asked.

Calpernicus nodded with a chuckle. "Damn all highborn Wolfryians."

"Killing the aristocracy would do nothing more than put their riches in your pocket," Tersius said.

Calpernicus winked. "True."

"Greed is the root of all evil, you know?" Tersius said.

Calpernicus inched closer to him and said, "No, boy. Greed ain't the root of all evil. The coin is a disruptor, but pride and ego are the real enemies. Pride tells me I can, and ego tells me I must."

"I still don't understand why everyone rebelled. I want to know," Tersius said.

Calpernicus chuckled and then smirked.

"So, what is the Rebellium planning on doing?" Tersius asked.

"Fighting as always." He pushed himself to his feet. "But we're not doing anything until your uncle comes back. Without his help, I would never question Valentinian's command," he replied.

"How does Valentinian fit into all this?" Tersius asked.

"Valentinian? He was Octavius's tutor early in life. He said that Octavius was pure of heart until his father's death." Calpernicus tapped his chin with his index finger and made eye contact with Tersius. "I think every man changes once his father dies. So, after Tiberius declared war on the world, Valentinian turned on him and formed the council. The council has the final say on all matters," Calpernicus said.

"Who joins the council?" Tersius asked.

"Men and women who were part of the Wolfryian senatore class. But they gave up their titles and joined Valentinian."

"Are you on the council?" Tersius asked.

Calpernicus chuckled. "Hell no, I'm not of noble birth. Some things will never change, no matter how many die for this cause. Valentinian is our *emperor* now," Calpernicus said, rolling his eyes as he walked away.

CHAPTER

Fourteen

Viridius gazed through the bars and watched the two guards closest to their cage as they slept. Once the festivities subsided, and the alcohol had taken effect, Viridius made his move.

The key to their salvation slid out of his tunic, and he inserted it into the lock. Giving the lock a quick twist, the gate swung open with a loud groan. Viridius froze and scanned the camp, his fingers wrapped around the cold, metal bars. A warrior urinated out the front of his tent, glanced in their direction, and then went back inside.

"That was close," Trakuta muttered, creeping up beside Viridius.

"You can say that again," Viridius said, trying to control the heartbeat pounding in his ears.

"Well, it's now or never. Lead the way," Trakuta whispered.

Viridius, Trakuta, Nigol, and two of Corcundia's men snuck to the first fire and pressed themselves firmly against the ash-covered boulders.

Nigol peered over the boulder and motioned for the others to follow him. "Those are the first two guards," he said, pointing at the nearest fire. "The next one has two more warriors." He pointed at a red tent. "Once you get past them, the tent you're looking for is right there," Nigol said.

"All right, everyone ready?" Viridius asked.

He scanned their faces as they nodded, the soot mingling with the sweat pooling around their eyes.

Viridius locked eyes with Trakuta, who asked, "Where do you need me?"

"I need you to take Corcundia's men and kill the guards around the fires and then follow me into the tent, get her, and then ride through the ravine."

Trakuta nodded and flashed him a quick smile. "See you at the rallying point," he said, slithering into the darkness, his silhouette nearly invisible.

"Where do I need to be?" Nigol asked.

Viridius took a moment and scanned the horse pens. He looked at their horses mixed in with a larger breed of animals the Ba warriors rode known as alpurlics. He could make out quite a few of the alpurlics in the darkness, but only a few of their horses. He couldn't see behind the alpurlics. Their massive white manes were too high.

Focusing again at his task at hand, Viridius said, "Go back to the cage and make sure my men have what they need," he whispered, checking his throwing knives. "Find every horse you can. If we lack horses, we die. Can you do it?"

Nigol bowed. "Of course, m'lord."

"Go," Viridius said.

He watched Nigol disappear and then turned his attention to the guards. He smiled as he watched Trakuta's feet fall silently in the sand. Once Trakuta's group reached the first fire, they slipped into the shadows. Viridius saw the flames illuminating the blade of his knife clenched between his teeth. Reaching the first guard, Trakuta slid under the tree trunk that his targets were using for a pillow.

Viridius watched Trakuta take a deep breath and hold it. The time between the warriors' snores grew longer as he slid his blade under one of the guard's large head. In the time it took to blink, Trakuta slammed the blade into the warrior's brain stem. His eyes opened wide, and droplets of blood fell out of his nostrils and onto the sand.

Trakuta smiled to himself, then turned his head and rolled to the next guard. The warrior was snoring so loudly he woke himself up. The guard sat up, sniffed a few times, then lay back down. Trakuta waited for the opportunity to strike, his thin blade catching the moonlight. Keeping focused, he slid his blade across the warrior's jugular. A third guard stepped up to the fire and urinated. Viridius gagged as he watched urine drip off Trakuta's face.

That's the worst—Ba piss. That musty smell won't come out of his clothes, Viridius thought.

The guard paused, looked around, and noticed the blood on the ash. He sniffed the air and then turned his head to alienate the smell coursing through his nostrils. Reaching for a horn strapped to his side, the warrior suddenly groaned and fell to his knees. His body pitched forward and landed face-first into the fire. Burnt fur wafted through Trakuta's nostrils as he yanked the warrior out of the fire.

Viridius sprinted past Trakuta, freeing both daggers from his belt. He snuck up on the next two guards, their snores covering his movements. Timing their breathing, Viridius placed both daggers across their throats simultaneously. He exhaled and slit them at the same time. Nodding his head at Trakuta, he crouched low and sprinted toward the tent housing Corcundia.

Under his breath, Trakuta muttered. "Show off."

Corcundia's men waited by the flaps of the tent as Trakuta and Viridius joined them.

"Here's the plan." He pointed at Corcundia's men. "You two keep a lookout for any other warriors. If you see one, caw like a crow, then disappear into the shadows."

Viridius flipped a knife in his palm and handed it to Trakuta. "Wait a few seconds after I enter the tent and then come in after me. If it ain't with us, it dies. Understand?" Viridius asked.

Trakuta nodded, the faint hint of a smile at the corner of his mouth. "No problem."

Viridius lay down on his stomach, preparing to crawl the ten yards to the tent. The steel from the knife between his teeth tasted gritty as he bit down on it. He crawled hand over fist to the entrance of the tent. It was deathly quiet. Nothing moved as he crept further in.

No warriors . . . that's unusual.

He saw Lady Corcundia lying facedown on a wide wooden bench, her feet and wrists bound, and her mouth gagged. Blood trickled from her scalp as Viridius stared at her, looking for signs of life. His heart sank. She didn't appear to be breathing. He crawled to where she was and saw the Ba warrior who had protected her against Dro'ka bound to a rack with leather straps covering his limbs. Rising to his knees, Viridius glanced over his shoulder and saw Trakuta slide in on his stomach behind him.

Viridius stood up and crept over to Corcundia, cut her bindings, and brushed the hair from the side of her face. Both of her eyes were blackened, and her hair was matted with blood. One of her eyes flickered open, and a weak smile crossed her lips.

"If it ain't my hired muscle," she whispered.

"You owe me money, and I plan to collect, but first, let's get you out of here," he said, surveying her wounds.

"I need to help him," she said, lifting her head in the direction of the torture rack.

"Like hell we do, he's dea—"

"I'm still alive, human. At least temporarily," K'aro grunted, thanking Trakuta as he helped him up.

"What the hell are you doing, Trakuta?"

"What? He helped her. I'm just returning the favor. What's right is right," Trakuta said, searching the room for anything that wasn't nailed down.

Staring into K'aro's one eye, Viridius muttered, "One move in the wrong direction or I think you aren't playing with straight dice, beast, I'll kill ya, and then wear you like a blanket."

K'aro chuckled. "If you feel like dying for no reason other than your foolish pride, human, I suggest you step closer."

Viridius stood silently, weighing his options.

Mirthlessly, K'aro said, "It is as I thought it would be. Shall we move past your childish threats and escape from here?" he asked as Trakuta helped him don his armor.

"Get them out of here, Trakuta, and ride for the rallying point. You two stay with me," Viridius said, pointing at Corcundia's men.

Trakuta carried Corcundia over his shoulder and half-dragged K'aro out behind him. A few moments later, a horn outside the tent shattered the cold, crisp air awakening the whole camp. Running to the entrance, Viridius watched Trakuta, Corcundia, and K'aro mount the horses Nigol brought them. He waited for Nigol to lead them into the darkness. The group disappeared as the camp swarmed to life. Roars echoed around them as the warriors got their bearings. Viridius and Corcundia's men stood in the shadows, their breath easy to see in the air.

A group of young warriors rode past them on their alpurlics, the beasts so dangerously close, they could have given away their hiding places. Viridius's back stiffened, and he held his breath until they rode by.

"Looks like they made it out of here," whispered one of Corcundia's men.

"Yea, now it's your turn," Viridius said.

Nigol left Whispers and two other horses' bridles tied by the entrance of Dro'ka's tent for them. Corcundia's men wasted no time and ran to untie their horses.

"You must provide backup for us," Viridius said from behind them.

The men spun around. "No, we don't! We ride with you to protect Lady Corcundia," shouted one of her men.

"You *are* helping her," Viridius said.

Like a bolt of lightning, Viridius slashed both of the men's Achilles' tendons. Their screams of anguish drew the warriors in their direction. Viridius tied the other two horses to his saddle and then mounted Whispers. As he galloped off into the darkness, Corcundia's men's screams were suddenly cut short.

"Cold as ice, m'lord," Nigol said, reining his horse in when Viridius finally caught up with them.

Viridius smiled. "Oh well, the only life that counts is mine."

"How long do we have?" Trakuta asked.

"Not sure, but we best be going," Viridius said.

"We have a few moments, m'lord. I took something they need and left them a surprise," Nigol said, holding something up in the dark.

"What ya got there?" Viridius asked.

Nigol threw him the locking pin to the horse pen, swung his horse around with a nod, and joined the rest of the men riding away. Viridius smiled at the item in his hand.

Cheeky son of a bitch. He is worth somet—

A huge explosion scattered the alpurlics and Viridius's thoughts. The blast killed a few of the warriors trying to round up the mounts for the warriors to ride out. A light chuckle could be heard behind him as he watched the chaotic scene from the shadows. Viridius glared at Aksutamoon, who had chuckled.

"What?" Viridius demanded.

"Now we're in for it. You killed their mounts. They will cut us into little bits and put us in the food they serve to the slaves," Aksutamoon said.

"Hell with them," Viridius said, turning his back to the king.

"Now, where do we go?" Viridius asked himself, scanning the night sky for the True Star. The sound of hooves approached from behind. Viridius pulled his sword and swung Whispers around.

"Help you with something?" Viridius asked, eyeing K'aro, who had ridden up behind him.

"Perhaps. If you want to survive, follow me," K'aro said more as an order than a request.

"Ha, that'll be the day. You're lucky to be breathing through your nostrils or whatever those are and not a hole in your windpipe. I will not follow a beast," Viridius said.

"He almost died protecting me, Viridius, and he became a slave in the process. At least he has honor. You, on the other hand, are low-life scum and owe me two men," Corcundia said, joining the conversation, her face flushed.

"Those men volunteered to stay behind, Corcundia," Viridius exclaimed.

"I watched from a looking glass, you bastard," she said coldly, handing the looking glass back to K'aro.

Viridius growled at K'aro. "I did what needed—"

Flexing her palm a few times rapidly, Corcundia concentrated on Viridius's face. He began to choke and spit, then looked around nervously. His swollen tongue pushed his lips apart as he scratched at his constricted larynx. His sight became hazy as he stared at her,

172 | D.B. BRAY with WAHIDA CLARK

wondering what else he could do. Gasping repeatedly, he fell from Whisper's back and rolled around on the ground.

"Never kill any of my men again," she said, staring down at him, tightening her grip. "Do I make myself clear?"

K'aro placed his paw on her shoulder and said, "Enough, m'lady. There is no honor in killing thieves."

A bloodred tear fell from the corner of her eye as she loosened her grip. She whistled at her remaining men and rode off behind K'aro. Air flooded into Viridius's oxygen-starved lungs as he gasped.

What in the hell was that?

Trakuta and Aksutamoon extended their arms, guffawing at him.

"So, shall I make dinner plans with her, or should you?" Trakuta asked with a chuckle.

Viridius cleared his throat and spat. "I'll kill that woman before our trip is out, mark my words," he said.

Viridius heard Gius groan as he woke up. He thought about leaving him behind after he was unconscious, but he still needed to get paid. It would be useless trying to get his money from the Rebellium council without Gius being there.

Nigol had ridden with Gius draped across his legs for quite a while without complaint. And after they stopped for a moment, Gius fell off the saddle and plummeted into the sand. He rolled over and sat up, taking in his surroundings.

He squinted at everyone in front of him and shouted, "Someone take these bindings off of me, now!"

Viridius motioned for Nigol to untie him. Gius scrambled to his feet and stormed up to Viridius.

"I demand a sword and shield to settle this in combat," Gius shrieked.

Viridius chuckled. "No time. We've been attempting an escape while you've been napping."

Gius stammered for a few minutes. His face flushed red, hands shaking. "I'm going to kill you. I don't care if we need you to kill the emperor or not."

"We'll fight later, Gius. Now, we need to escape, but I'll kill you when we get to the Rebellium's campsite, if you wish," Viridius said dismissively over his shoulder, mounting Whispers.

"Nigol, give him a horse of his own and follow me," Viridius said as he rode off.

Their company followed K'aro as he led them deeper into the Lava Lands. A lake of lava appeared on the horizon in front of them, its heat cascading over them. An ash storm, similar to a sandstorm, swirled around them as they galloped across the valley until their horses began to slow.

"If we don't rest soon, these horses will die," Trakuta said, peering into the ash behind them.

A horse near Viridius reared up on its hindquarters with a screech and fell over.

"Cover!" Viridius shouted.

The rider shouted in pain from underneath the dead horse, half his body pinned to the ash. Trakuta rushed to the soldier's aid and tried to pull the dead carcass off of him. As he bent down, an arrow buzzed by his head and cut the man's screams short. The rest of their group dismounted as another horse slammed headfirst into the gray ash, throwing its rider. A long, thin arrow protruded from the horse's thick mane.

"Where did that come from?" shouted a voice as the group formed, backs to one another.

Shadows loomed above them, their large bows strung. K'aro stepped out from the group and sprinted up a path to the top of the ravine.

"If I catch you, coward, I'll gut you!" Viridius bellowed, freeing his sword.

As soon as the shadows appeared, they disappeared. Viridius shouted for his group to form two rows. "Front rank, kneel. Second rank, nock drawstrings."

"Wait for the command," Trakuta shouted, stepping in front of Aksutamoon.

K'aro reemerged from the pathway with his fist closed above his head. Corcundia tried to leave the group, but Viridius snatched her by her shoulder.

"Oi, you still owe me money," he said.

Corcundia glanced at his hand and then raised her other hand. "Do we have a problem?"

Shit . . . He withdrew his hand. "Nope. No problem."

K'aro led a small group from the path and met with Corcundia and her men in the middle of the ravine. Viridius watched the exchange and wrapped his sweaty fingers around the hilt of his sword. He watched K'aro's movements closely and made eye contact with Trakuta.

"I'm going to see what's going on. Something doesn't feel right. Keep an arrow aimed at my back, Trakuta. If there's trouble, I'll fall back with her. Order the men to kill whatever may be chasing me," Viridius said.

"Don't be a hero," Trakuta muttered, nocking an arrow.

Smiling wide, Viridius said, "Never happen."

Viridius walked with a sense of purpose to the exchange. As he approached the warriors in front of him, an arrow slammed in front of his next step. Glancing down at the arrow, Viridius dropped to a knee and pulled it from the ash. He slid the arrow under his nose and smelled it.

Ah, pine resin. No other smell like it.

He stood up. "I'm Viridius Vispanius. I'm with Lady Corcundia. Don't shoot."

He raised his hands above his head and walked the last few feet to Corcundia. He gave K'aro a cold stare, the hatred burning from his eye sockets. K'aro shook his mane and then continued to speak to the cloaked figure next to him in deep guttural growls. Puzzled, Viridius watched them talk, and his eyes drifted over to Corcundia. Nigol ambled up behind him and said, "Careful with the words you use here, m'lord. These be the monsters every Ba warrior fears. They loathe slaves."

"I'm no man's slave, Nigol. And that's enough out of you," Viridius hissed, pushing him back.

K'aro moved his hand in Viridius's direction and made a few gestures. The figure K'aro was speaking with gave a low, growling laugh.

Viridius glanced at Nigol, who translated, "K'aro of the Runners told them—"

"What?" Viridius demanded.

Nigol lowered his head.

Viridius cut his eyes at Nigol. "Last chance before it gets messy in here," Viridius said, sliding his palm to his sword hilt.

Pushing his arm down, Nigol said, "Wait, m'lord, wait. He said you would make a good wife."

Viridius never lost a step as he ran into K'aro full-on. The unexpected blow broke several of K'aro's ribs. Roaring, K'aro chomped down on Viridius's arm as they rolled around in the ash. Viridius shouted in pain as teeth broke through his skin. He cursed at K'aro and landed two solid blows on the side of his furry ear. K'aro roared again and applied more pressure to Viridius's arm. Someone grabbed Viridius by the back of the neck and launched him a few feet away into the ash.

He got to his feet and rotated the pommel of his sword in his palm. "You crazy cat thing. I'm no one's wife! No one's, you hear me! When I get my hands around that furry neck, I'm going to squeeze it till your head pops off!" He charged forward again, sword raised. A kick from the side knocked the air from his chest. He landed on his back with a loud groan.

Shit.

He could hear the sounds of men rushing by him, but he could only gasp as he attempted to catch his breath. Two ranks formed in front of him led by King Aksutamoon.

"Rank one, advance on the double. Second rank, hold here!" Trakuta shouted.

Waving her hands in front of her face, Corcundia held both groups at bay.

"King Aksutamoon, back down, now! They're allies," she shouted.

"Unlikely, love. I don't much like the dark-skinned man in the ash, but I like that lion thing even less," he said, sliding his bastard sword from the scabbard strapped across his back. He stepped over Viridius in a defensive position, his sword held high above his head. Trakuta crossed his blades in front of his chest as he stepped in front of Aksutamoon.

"Wait!" K'aro roared, holding his side with one paw, the other outstretched. "These are The Outkast. They are the sworn enemies of the Runners, and the other Ba prides."

The warriors behind K'aro untied their red scarves, revealing their scarred faces. Some were missing incisors or clumps of fur. A large eye was branded onto their right wrists, identifying them as having lost their honor. They were warriors convicted of heinous crimes against their fellow warriors, with crimes ranging from adultery with a shield brother's wife to fratricide and patricide. Trakuta helped Viridius to his feet, who coughed, cleared his throat, and then nodded his thanks. He turned his attention back to the warriors and arched his back.

"So, which of these things says I'll make a good wife?"

"Wife? No one said wife, human. I said warrior— warrior!" K'aro roared, putting pressure on his side.

Nigol cleared his throat nervously and stared at the ash. Viridius chuckled as he walked up to him. He raised his chin and glared into his eyes. "Explain," he hissed.

Nigol chuckled nervously and said, "Um, those two words are very—"

Viridius headbutted Nigol and sent him crashing into the ash. Trakuta walked up and grabbed Nigol by the feet and dragged him away.

Viridius watched them for a moment, then turned to K'aro. "My apologies. I thought my translator spoke your language."

"He does, but our words differ from pride to pride. The slave Nigol speaks D'atu. Not R'atu." K'aro pointed at the warrior next to him. "This is Aa'tu of the mighty R'atu. He only has half his tongue, so he's hard to understand," K'aro said, watching Nigol's head bounce up and down as it passed over mounds of ash.

"They were laughing at me being a great warrior. Why?" Viridius asked.

"You're a slave, nothing more. They have never seen a human take up arms," K'aro said.

"I'll show you a slave," Viridius said, stepping forward.

"Watch yourself, human," Aa'tu said in perfect Dellosian, raising a hand with a missing index finger.

White tips passed through Aa'tu's slicked back graying mane. Viridius noticed flesh missing throughout his body, lumps of pink scar tissue taking their place. An arrow thudded between them from the ridgeline.

"These are my lands," Aa'tu said, pointing to the ridgeline. "*Not* yours."

Viridius spat at his padded feet, sheathed his sword, and raised his hands. "So be it."

A loud roar echoed into the ravine as one of The Outkast above them fell off the ridge and into the ash. His brain matter splattered across Viridius's worn boots as he landed. A deep horn blew as The Outkast prepared themselves for battle.

Roaring, K'aro yanked his sword from his side, then pointed to where he wanted Corcundia's men. "Archers to the back, spearmen to the front, calvary bring up the rear," K'aro said in Dellosian.

"I ain't fighting for you," Viridius said, stepping back.

"Then die," K'aro said, leading Corcundia and her men over to Aa'tu.

Goddammit, I don't want this.

As Viridius searched for an escape, Trakuta jogged past him with Aksutamoon and his men. "Aren't you leaving with me?" Viridius asked.

Turning his head, Trakuta smiled. "No, no, those bastards over that ridge got plenty of treasure on them. I'm going to get mine and eat until I'm suckled like a sow."

Viridius stared at his boots and wrapped his hand around the hilt of his sword.

I'm going to regret this, I just know it. I'm nobody's hero, he thought as he charged after Trakuta.

CHAPTER

Fifteen

Sweat dripped from Tersius's brow as he scanned the encampment. The smell of shit after a night of drinking made him throw up into the cold blue water. Knees skinned from a fall earlier, he lifted his head with a groan, hoping no one had seen him. As he straightened himself, he wiped his tunic sleeve across his sunburnt lips.

"I'm never drinking again," he muttered, holding his head in his hands.

Casting a shadow over him, surrounded by guards, Valentinian said, "When you're done acting like a child, Tersius, I would like to see you in my tent."

Sluggishly, Tersius stumbled behind him, head lowered. Valentinian was always the stalwart leader of the Rebellium, but the years hadn't been kind to him. With his eyesight nearly gone and walking with a limp, he knew it was only a matter of time before he would not rise one day soon. Octavius had to die before he did.

The closer they got to Valentinian's tent, the more Tersius's mind raced. Looking around, he felt the hairs on the back of his neck stand on end. It only lasted a moment, then left. They crossed into the tent, and Valentinian held his hands by a candlewick that had burned down to the brass holder. Tersius looked around the inside of the tent. A globe of Dellos sat in a stand in one corner of the tent with tomes of books surrounding it. The tent was plain in every respect, except for the hundreds of books lining its walls. A straw bed and a basin of cold water were his only luxuries.

Calpernicus stood with a few of his men by an oak table in the opposite corner, poring over a battle map.

"Without Viridius, it can't be done," Calpernicus said to one of the burly men on his left.

Valentinian walked over to the table, crossed his arms over his chest, and took a deep breath. "Are you a Drathi*can* or a Drathi*cant*, Calpernicus?" Valentinian asked.

After hearing the question, Calpernicus's face reddened. He placed both palms on the table and leaned forward. "I am a true Drathi*can*, m'lord. And I have the scars to prove it."

"Then prove it."

Calpernicus fumed as he watched Valentinian walk away. He turned back to the map, grinding his teeth, and said, "If Viridius doesn't come, can it be done by someone else?"

One of his men paused and shrugged. "What . . . assassinate the emperor?"

Calpernicus sighed and rubbed his eyes. "Yes."

"No, m'lord. All our best are dead, remember? That's why we needed him in the first place," the commander said after taking a sip of wine.

"If our assassin doesn't show up soon with Gius, we will have to make a frontal assault. We have Asinius now who can open the gates for us. Lord Gius has been gone too long. He may have been killed by Viridius when he tried to recruit him. It is a chance that I cannot take with Asinius in the next tent. There isn't a moment to waste," Valentinian said from nearby, interrupting them.

Calpernicus grumbled and rubbed his red eyes, casually tracing the lines of Wolfryia on the map. His finger slid over the trees and mountains leading up to the city of Iceport. "I thought we would wait for Viridius so we could save our men's lives." He groaned before speaking. "And if we don't wait, it's going to get bloody, and many of ours will die needlessly. That was the whole point of recruiting Viridius."

"Don't pout, Calpernicus," Valentinian said as he spun his globe. He looked at Tersius and said, "What news of Asinius?"

"He tells me nothing."

Walking with his hands clasped behind his back, Valentinian spoke out loud. "It doesn't matter. We will kill the emperor all the same. My days are short in this world. How many we lose will be substantially higher than I first anticipated." He glanced at his cup, his eyes cold. "I will do anything to kill the emperor, no matter how many men I lose."

"M'lord, we have precious few remaining. How can you ask them to sacrifice more?" Calpernicus asked, stomping up to Valentinian from the table, his frustrations now not hidden beneath the surface.

Valentinian glanced up from his book, over the rim of his eyeglasses, then tapped his chin with a smirk and said, "Because I command them to die for the cause, and that includes *all* of you as well."

"My life is worth more than dying in a headlong assault, m'lord. Octavius will die, but not with my men's lives needlessly thrown away to make it happen," Calpernicus spat.

"I still command the power here. Know your place, Calpernicus. If I command it, it will be done. In fact, I want *your* men to lead the charge when we mobilize the army." The smudge from Valentinian's finger on the map smeared the area around Iceport, emphasizing his point. "Asinius will take us to the throne room after we breach the gate." Slamming his hand onto the map, Valentinian finished. "And I will kill Octavius. Well, I won't. Your men will. Are any of you stupid enough to challenge my authority?"

Calpernicus lowered his head and muttered, "No, m'lord, but why rush? We have lived this long by being cautious. We should wait longer for Lord Gius."

Valentinian chuckled, rolled his eyes, and looked over at Tersius and mouthed, "Cowards."

A slave with an olive complexion, black hair, and leathery skin approached Valentinian and filled his cup. Valentinian's hand slid over the rim of the goblet, and he swallowed the contents. He licked his lips. "I need something stronger. Tersius, bring me my favorite drink." He pointed to the table.

"What's your plan, m'lord?" Tersius asked, handing him the lead goblet.

With his goblet full of Tears of Tramonia, Valentinian took a sip, adjusted his spectacles, and said, "When we bring Asinius aboard, he will help us by opening the gates. No more waiting." Valentinian burped lightly, then tapped his chest. He stared at the goblet. "This whiskey has gone south. Shouldn't waste it, though," he said, pouring more into his glass.

The sound of Valentinian clearing his throat was raspy, almost allergic sounding. He smacked his lips together, glanced at the goblet, then dropped it. "No use wasting good whiskey. My, I feel . . . . I feel peculiar. As I was say—" Valentinian said, swallowing hard as he sank to his knees.

Dropping to catch him, Calpernicus held him as the first convulsions coursed through his body. A bloody froth exploded from his mouth, covering Tersius. He sat up and vomited dark pools of blood. "It's not supposed—"

"Get the healer!" one of the men shouted.

Calpernicus held Valentinian as the guards rushed in with a physician. He pointed at Tersius and yelled, "He killed our lord! Capture him."

Tersius held his hands up. "Whoa. I had nothing to do with it. I've been with you in this tent the whole time. How dare you accuse me of this crime."

Valentinian frantically opened a book by his hand and ripped out a page. He thrust it into Tersius's pocket, gasping for breath. His chest heaved, and his head snapped side to side like a teeter-totter. So much to say, so little time. Valentinian opened his mouth, tried to say something, but nothing came out. His chest stilled, and the blood gurgling in his throat subsided. Calpernicus lowered him onto the ground and glared at Tersius with watery eyes.

Reaching his feet, Calpernicus squared his jaw and said, "Tersius of Drathia, you are charged with killing Lord Valentinian, ruler of the Rebellium. Guards, take him to a holding cell until his trial in the morning."

The physician inspected the blood flowing from Valentinian's nostrils and right eye. He knelt beside the body and stuck his finger inside Valentinian's mouth and pulled it back out. Lifting the blood to the tip of his tongue, he tasted it, then vigorously spat on the ground. "Ach, poison."

"Bring all the slaves that were in this tent," he hissed to another commander in the room.

Calpernicus's men chased down the slaves who served Valentinian in the last week and brought them back to the tent. Calpernicus lined them up and assigned guards to interrogate them. He noticed a thin man with black hair easing his way out of the tent as the guards selected the other slaves.

"Stop him!" Calpernicus shouted.

Tersius shook off his guard's grip and turned to stop the man. The assassin's blade bit into Tersius's neck, snapping off at the hilt in the process as he sprinted by. A guard overreacted and thrust his long spear into the assassin's stomach, disemboweling him.

In a fit of rage, Calpernicus drew his sword. "You idiot," he shouted, swinging his sword at the man's neck, cutting it wide open. The dead guardsman's long spear clattered to the dirt. Calpernicus's men and Valentinian's guards squared off in the cramped quarters, weapons at the ready.

"Now, there's more than one way out of this, and bloodshed can be avoided," Calpernicus shouted.

A guard tentatively stepped forward and stabbed at Calpernicus in response, barely missing him. "Nightshades," Calpernicus roared.

Calpernicus's personal guards, The Nightshades, rushed in and took Valentinian's guards from behind, quickly putting them to the sword. Calpernicus spat on a nearby body as one of his men carried Tersius's limp form from the tent. One of The Nightshades' commanders walked up to Calpernicus.

"What are your orders, m'lord?"

Calpernicus sighed and wiped the gore from his stained blade. "Prepare Lord Valentinian for cremation, clean the bodies up, and let the men know our leader is deceased. I will take command until Lord Gius returns with Viridius."

The commander nodded as Calpernicus stepped over Valentinian's warm corpse and returned to studying the map of Iceport.

Marus peered through his grubby telescopic lens, blinked, then refocused as he tried to make out the violent scene transpiring below them. Everything had gone as planned, and he never stepped foot in the camp. Valentinian appeared to have been killed and with him, their worthless cause. A shadow snuck up to his outcropping and grunted with strained effort.

"I'm gettin' too old for this shit," Marus's companion said.

Marus nodded, ignored the man, and then stared back down his spyglass. Squinting downrange without a spyglass, he saw the figure excitedly raised his hand and said, "This is the perfect time to attack, m'lord."

Marus yanked the man's arm down with a glare and returned to what he was doing. If anything, Zillas, his companion, was more of a liability than an asset. He drank too much wine, which made him impetuous, and a drunk man was a bad omen who cost soldiers their lives when they talked out of turn.

But he was Octavius's cousin and afforded the luxury of being a pain in the ass. During the suppression of the Rebellium, he was a great warrior and leader, but the Tears of Tramonia had transformed him. Zillas now ran errands for the commanders and went out with the scouting parties. Usually, the scouts brought him back over their shoulders.

As Marus scanned the cells, he saw an individual leaning against the bars in a torn white tunic and tan breeches. "It can't be . . ." Marus mumbled.

"What do you see?" Zillas asked.

"My unicorn," he replied.

"Your unicorn? What the hell does that mean?" Zillas asked, then hiccuped.

Marus cawed like a crow, and one of his men crawled to him. The new man lay flat on his stomach, waiting for a command from Marus. Marus handed the new man the spyglass, then rolled out of his way. The commander scanned the landscape and murmured, "It can't be that easy, can it?"

"What do you think, Precipitous?" Marus asked.

Snickering, Precipitous said, "That's him. I know that arrogant stance anywhere. I can't believe he got caught by the rebels. Serves him right, though." He glanced over at Marus with a shrug. "So, why do we need to intervene?"

Marus growled. "Because I want his head. But no one moves from this bluff until I give the order. Once I get Asinius, kill everyone else in the camp, but not before."

"Don't let your hate get you killed or miss an opportunity the emperor insists on being done, m'lord," Precipitous warned.

"When I want your recommendations, I'll give them to you, Precipitous," Marus spat.

Precipitous paused, cut his eyes at him, and then shook his head. "You, and what army, Prefect? Have you already forgotten what happened in the dungeon with the emperor?"

Precipitous had followed Marus through the Rebellium Wars and, in the process, lost his right wrist, courtesy of a Ba warrior. He also carried a single jagged scar that ran across his leathery face at an angle.

"Remember, Marus. I've saved your ass more times than you can count on your fingers and toes. You want to talk to Zillas like that, do it. He's a drunken bastard, but watch how you speak to me," Precipitous said, handing Marus the spyglass.

Precipitous waited for Marus's response and stared into his troubled eyes. Marus's lip twitched at his comment. He rolled away and then walked back to the campfire.

"I don't think that was what he expected from you," Zillas said with a drunk giggle.

"I don't care. Marus is quick to see red and stupid enough to do something irrational. Now, I won't start trouble, but should he need me to finish it, I will," Precipitous said.

"Does that mean kicking him when he's down?"

Precipitous cut his eyes at him. "My emperor commands, I follow."

"I bet, and if I didn't know you any better, I would say you were plotting on him," Zillas hissed.

Staring intently at the men rushing to the tent, Precipitous spoke out the side of his mouth. "And that's why you'll always be a runner and an errand boy. You're nowhere near the warrior you used to be. So leave the thinking to me, Drunk."

Zillas grinned at the slight and tipped his bottle toward Precipitous. The pair waited in silence, wiping the sweat from their faces. Precipitous waited patiently as he watched the valley floor. The tent they had seen Valentinian enter and exit from had blood smeared across the opening. Someone dragged a limp, bloody body out of the tent and tossed it into Asinius's cell. Precipitous didn't recognize the man's face, nor did he care. He knew a surprise attack would destroy them, but if he didn't follow Marus's order, he would be executed along with any rebel survivors.

Precipitous and Zillas snuck back to their camp and sat by Marus, who was slowly chewing on a piece of raw meat. He ground it between his teeth and glared at them as they approached. He took a sip from his wineskin, then handed it across the smoldering fire to Precipitous as he sat down. Hesitating for a moment, Precipitous reached for it against his better judgment. Then Marus dropped it into a pile of horse shit beside them.

"Prick," Precipitous mumbled.

"That and worse—much worse," Marus said with a smirk.

The other members of their small raiding party came and sat down beside them after they returned from their scouting mission. Marus picked up a stick at his feet, sharpened it, and picked his teeth.

Sucking his bleeding gums, Marus said, "So, what's the plan, Precipitous? Since you think you're the mighty general."

Precipitous shrugged and grabbed a rock from the ground. "How should I know? It's your command."

Marus glanced across the fire at the scouts he sent out. "What did you men see?" he asked, turning his attention away from Precipitous.

"The only way in is a frontal assault unless you send someone in to unlock the gate from the inside. It would take several towers that we will need to build to breach that wall," the tired leader responded.

Marus nodded. "I think—"

Precipitous cut him off. "Emperor Octavius commands Asinius's head. We need to go tonight, Lord Marus—damn the cost."

Marus slapped Precipitous across the face for cutting him off. "Do . . . not . . . interrupt . . . me . . . again," he said with emphasis, staring into his eyes.

Precipitous yanked a blade from his forearm and swung it at Marus's neck for striking him. A sword swung out of the shadows of the bonfire and struck his wooden hand, knocking it off. It was followed by a fist and a vicious knee to the temple. The stars danced around Precipitous's head for a moment, and then he fell to the ground. Zillas stood by Marus and nodded at him.

Marus waved his hand dismissively, ignoring the fact that Zillas had saved his life. "Take him and his hand away. I will punish him when he wakes up."

Marus waited while Precipitous was dragged away and then continued. "As I was saying before I was rudely interrupted, we will pull back and get the rest of our army, and once we have reassembled both legions, we will return. I need a volunteer to surrender to their patrols and then reach my man on the inside who can unlock the gate for us. Any volunteers?" he asked.

One of his scouts raised an eyebrow and cleared his throat. "You have a man on the inside, m'lord?"

"I do," Marus stated.

"Why do one of ours need to reach him, then?"

"Because I want the gate opened quickly, and I don't want to wait for him to come to us," he spat. "I want our calvary through the gate first, followed by our legionnaires. Once we're in, slaughter everyone. So, who's my volunteer?" Marus asked.

Marus knew none of his men would go; it was too risky. If the person were discovered, they would be tortured and killed. He scanned the group assembled and saw his chance to get rid of Zillas.

"Zillas, you will surrender," Marus stated, after taking another sip of wine.

"Wait a hot damn minute. I didn't volunteer," Zillas said with a hiccup.

"No, you didn't, but when your cousin finds out you did, he will probably promote you to prefect. You up for it?" Marus asked.

"You really think he would do that?" Zillas asked, both eyebrows raised.

"Of course, I do. I wouldn't have said it if I didn't think so. Get captured, then speak to my ally, and make sure he unlocks the gate."

"Who's your contact?" Zillas asked.

"When he recognizes you, he will reveal himself to you," Marus said.

Zillas nodded with a smile, grabbed a wineskin, and stumbled off alone into the darkness. His curses could be heard as he walked into something past the tree line. Marus felt along his neckline and drew blood from the wound Precipitous had given him.

"Rat bastard," he murmured.

One of Marus's men walked up and began sewing the wound using dirty fingers. "Clean your hands," Marus hissed, slapping him away. "You want me to die from an infection?"

The man paused and washed his hands with wine. He glanced up at Marus. "Do you really believe what you just said, Prefect Marus?"

"Of course, I don't, but Zillas doesn't know that, and if he dies, Octavius will burn Dellos to the ground in retribution. After all, his son is Octavius's spawn."

The healer's jaw dropped.

"Come, man, you didn't know?" Marus asked. He took a swig of wine. "I mean, Octavius did impregnate Zillas's wife." Marus exhaled deeply. "I can't believe he fucked his sister . . . yuk." He chuckled. "And that idiot Zillas actually believes Zactus is from his loins. Learn this fact about Octavius. He's a real bastard, but the real problem for Dellos is *hope*. The Rebellium scum still believes in hope, and hope is more dangerous than any weapon or torture device. Men will sacrifice their lives for a cause like that."

The point of Marus's knife scraped across one of the rocks in the fire pit. He stared into the sky, his breath catching the cool night air. "Ach, Zillas's a worthless drunk anyway, and either he's too stupid or too ignorant to know his wife had a child with another man. He would serve Wolfryia better by getting himself killed during his capture."

"I see your point, Prefect," the healer said softly.

Marus's eyes scanned the campfire and noticed he was the only one left. "Leave me," Marus said to his healer.

"As you wish, m'lord."

Marus stood, brushed himself off, and then walked toward his tent for a few hours of sleep.

CHAPTER

Sixteen

An arrow twice the length of a human one snapped by Viridius's face and thudded into the back of the man behind him.

Damn, that was close.

He watched Dro'ka throw his bow to the ground, bare his incisors, and then mount his silver and blue alpurlic.

"Hold the line," Trakuta shouted, pulling his drawstring back and firing two arrows high into the sky. He shoved the men around him to their knees and stood behind them, continuously firing. "Easy, boys, easy," he shouted, encouraging them.

One of his arrows struck one of the warriors next to Dro'ka, tumbling him from the saddle as they rode hard across the ravine floor.

"Nice shot," Viridius said.

"I was aiming for that guy," Trakuta said, pointing at Dro'ka as he strung his bow and fired another arrow. "I hate getting old. My eyes aren't what they used to be." He turned his head toward his archers. "On my command."

He watched Dro'ka's warriors close the gap. "Loose!" He glanced at Viridius after giving his command. "So, you with me, or are you running?"

"I'm here, aren't I?" Viridius hissed, picking up two spears at his feet. He slammed one of the spears into the ground and shouted, "First line, brace shields. Second line, spears at the ready."

Trakuta smiled as he watched Viridius readying the men.

"See you in the afterlife," Trakuta shouted to Viridius.

A volley of arrows landed among the defenders, killing several men caught in the open. The D'atu roared as they galloped faster across the ash. Some of the Tramonians turned to flee, pushing past The Outkast as Dro'ka blew on his horn.

Aksutamoon rode in front of his men as they retreated. He held his hands up and stood up in his stirrups, the fat on his underarms shaking. "Tramonians . . . Tramonians, hear me! Return and die with your fellows. Are you true Tramonians or cowards?" he bellowed above the din of battle.

Most of the men stopped. Only a few continued by him. The Outkast near them turned, fired, and killed the men who made it past Aksutamoon. The man who stopped stared at Aksutamoon mounted on his chestnut mare, the Tramonian flag fluttering by his side. There was nothing special about the plain red flag with a brown barrel of wine on it, but his men would die for it.

"Come with me! Who will come with me?" he roared as he slammed his visor down, the sun reflecting off of it. He yanked the reins on his mount, standing it up on its hind legs. A few of his men gave halfhearted cheers and returned to the line.

Viridius saw Gius and Nigol walking toward the line. A soldier carrying spears and arrows knocked Gius down as he rushed to rejoin his comrades. Viridius yanked Gius up by the nape of his neck, untied his rope bindings, and shoved a sword into his hands.

"Fight or die, Gius. Your choice."

"If we survive this, Viridius, watch what you eat and drink."

"You haven't got the balls," Viridius said with a sneer. "Remember, old friend, you need me more than I need you."

"A weapon, please, m'lord," Nigol said, approaching from Viridius's left.

"Can you fight?" Viridius asked with a wide smile.

Nigol shook his head no. Viridius turned to Nigol and tossed him a spear. "Be careful out there. If we don't meet again, thank you for freeing us."

Nigol nodded with a small smile, then ambled to the front line, his hunchback lowered as far as it could behind one of the Tramonian's shields. Viridius glanced at Gius with contempt.

"See you in hell," he said, then strode toward the first line of defenders.

The D'atu rode eight across as they thundered through the valley. Row after row of Dro'ka's warriors bore down on them, even as they fell from the barrage of arrows.

K'aro slid his blade across his forearm and forced the blood onto the ash. He calmly said in Dellosian, "I have protected you with the blood of the Ba spirits. Have no fear. Spears at the ready, archers; nock." He heard the click of the arrows as they were pulled against their bowstrings. "Loose!"

Their arrows flew downrange and slammed into both warrior and beast. Howls of pain could be heard from the warriors mixed with screeches from the alpurlics. Aksutamoon's men cheered and then watched in horror as the D'atu rode over their dead and wounded. Groans could be heard up and down the line as they watched them continue on.

A warrior missing an ear stood near Viridius and roared an order in Dellosian. "Brace!"

The R'atu, led by Aa'tu, sprinted in front of the Tramonian lines in a wedge formation, their red scarves fluttering behind them. Aa'tu scanned his warriors' faces, then back glanced back at Viridius.

"Human, they say you can fight. I doubt it, but if by chance, you are a warrior, prove me wrong."

K'aro walked up to Viridius and picked a target, fired, and blasted an attacking warrior out of his saddle. Viridius smirked and looked at both Aa'tu and K'aro. He spat at their feet and then pulled his bowstring to his chin. Never breaking Aa'tu's gaze, he smiled arrogantly and fired his arrow.

Dro'ka caught the arrow as it descended, snapped it in half, and threw it to the ground. Viridius wasn't sure, but he thought he heard him laughing as he rode over the last bit of ash. Dro'ka snatched a javelin from the side of his saddle and threw it along with the other riders. Instinctively, Gius pushed Viridius to the ground as Dro'ka's javelin slammed into a shield behind them. Viridius looked up and spat out a mouthful of ash.

Gius smiled. "It must hurt that I'll always be smarter than you." He stepped over Viridius and engaged the D'atu.

Aa'tu yanked Viridius to his feet. "Let's get our glory!"

By all that's holy, that's the last time anyone knocks me to the ground.

A Tramonian commander shouted, "Loose!"

As more arrows flew from their lines, K'aro and Viridius sprinted toward The Outkast, who stood in two rows. The left row held their spears at an angle, their ten-foot oiled spearheads forming like rows of teeth. The tips gleamed in the orange volcanic light, a mix of obsidian and iron.

Staring straight-ahead, Viridius muttered under his breath, "I owe you, beast."

Aa'tu gave him a curt nod. "Start by calling me by my name, slave."

Viridius took a swig from a bottle he had hidden and sighed, "So, this is the end, eh, Aa'tu?"

Trakuta shouted beside them, "Give them everything you got. Loose!"

Aa'tu shook his mane at Viridius and smiled. "Nothing is ever as it seems." He raised his arm, a bright red sash flowing from his elbow. Fire arrows flew down from the ridgeline above, wiping out a group of D'atu riders at the back of the attacking column. Dro'ka's warriors were unable to rein their mounts in and crashed into the raised spears of The Outkast. The bodies of both warriors and alpurlics hung limp, impaled on the long shafts. Shouts and screams from the men, and screeches and agonizing roars reverberated through the ravine as the two groups collided.

The plethora of shouts, curses, roars, neighing horses, and roaring alpurlics made men clamp their teeth, some shattering their roots. Piles of intestines, blood, and shit were plentiful as the scene of carnage unfolded. The bodies of both friend and foe mixed together, the dead tripping the living as they continued their scramble for survival. A small group of humans formed a phalanx and surrounded Aksutamoon.

The phalanx surged forward around him, impaling the D'atu warriors as they crashed through the first spear line. Viridius watched Gius lead a few injured men to plug the gap in the center and then watched him disappear into the ash falling around them. As the Tramonians pushed the D'atu back, a large vase flew over the phalanx.

K'aro sniffed, his ears perking up. "Firepot!" he roared.

He bounded to one of The Outkast, who held his paws cupped near his knees. The warrior bent over at the waist and lifted K'aro into the sky. K'aro leaped, but a javelin tore into his helper's neck, slamming him to the ground. The javelin caught the back of K'aro's ankle, and he plummeted to the ground near the other dead warrior. K'aro, rising to his feet, felt two arrows thump into his armor. He dropped his spear and collapsed into the bloodstained ash.

A dismounted D'atu warrior roared, "Push!"

A few of the men in the phalanx retreated and left Aksutamoon vulnerable to attack. The king didn't seem to notice as he ran his sword through the warrior in front of him. He buried it up to the hilt and then lost control of the weapon as the warrior fell under his horse's hooves. He glanced around his saddlebag and pulled one of his spires.

Another D'atu warrior yanked on Aksutamoon's leg from below and held him still as another warrior galloped toward him and leaped from all fours. Viridius's arrow slammed into the leaping warrior's eye and sent him crashing to the ground. Aksutamoon hacked the other warrior's arm off, then lifted his sword and saluted Viridius.

Firepots exploded over the phalanx, melting most of Aksutamoon's men's heads. A cloud of black smoke and screams were all that remained of the Tramonians. The screeches of agony around Viridius echoed in his ears. As the number of humans in the fight dwindled, Aksutamoon ordered a retreat and was finally cut down from behind. Trakuta collapsed into the ash beside him as a D'atu warrior with one arm leaned over him with his sword raised.

Viridius searched madly for Corcundia and saw her across the battlefield. Sprinting through the mass of bodies, he slowed as the blood-soaked ground around him stopped his momentum. A young boy beat Viridius to Corcundia's side. A D'atu warrior nearby swung his sword at her as she wiped her soot-stained face. The young Tramonian boy stepped in front of the sword strike meant for her, then fell to the ash, his head split open.

As Viridius reached Corcundia, he lowered his shoulder and drove his sword into the warrior's back. Another warrior approached them and raised his spear over his head. A knife flew through the air and embedded into his attacker's throat. The warrior stumbled forward and fell on Viridius, crushing him to the ground. A horn pierced the air around them.

Can my life get any worse? Viridius thought.

Roars from the victorious D'atu could be heard drowning out the sounds of the humans screaming. Before his eyes closed, Viridius thought he saw red scarves coming down behind them. Then a massive paw thumped his skull.

CHAPTER

Seventeen

The pain in Viridius's head was excruciating. He felt the back of it and drew blood from a gash behind his right ear. A warrior knelt beside him and said, "You'll live. Get up, slave."

The smell of wet fur wafted into Viridius's nostrils again. He rolled over onto his back and sat up slowly. The bodies surrounding him were stacked like a dam in a river of blood. The limbs of both humans and Ba warriors were intermingled throughout the battlefield. After getting to his feet, Viridius put his hands on his knees and coughed.

That was a terrible idea. Should have run. I doubt anyone's alive.

A shadow appeared above him and spoke. "Don't expect me to say thank you. You still owe me two men."

Growling in anger, Viridius said, "Now, wait a minute. I saved your life, and this is the thanks I get?"

"You protected an investment, not me, personally," Corcundia said, walking away.

After he thought for a moment, Viridius went to speak but heard a neighing behind him and turned. Whispers lay mortally wounded near several D'atu corpses. Viridius pushed through the men around him and took a knee in front of his beloved horse.

"Easy boy, easy now," Viridius said, stroking his mane, his voice catching in his throat.

Whispers had only been with him for a short time, but he had loved again, no matter how brief. He clenched his teeth and lay his head on Whisper's neck, fighting back his tears. It was only a matter of time, and he was beginning to suffer.

I'm sorry it happened like this, boy. I wish we could have plowed fields and rode through pastures, but it never happens that way for me. Everything I touch dies or disappears. Why should this be any different?

Corcundia walked up behind him and cleared her throat. "You want us to help?"

His sword pierced Whisper's heart as she asked, silencing his pain. A single, salty tear fell onto his dirt-stained cheek, the first since the death of his wife.

"No. My horse, my problem," he whispered with a sigh.

He slowly lowered Whisper's head into the ash and slid his fingers over his eyelids.

Death . . . all this death. I hate the Ba. Nothing more than talking animals.

Whisper's death quieted those around him. Men and warriors lay wounded side by side, moaning, the dead frozen in one last desperate act of defiance.

"What the hell happened?" Viridius asked, spitting blood onto the ground and wiggling one of his teeth.

Corcundia spoke. "I'm sorry about—"

Staring straight-ahead, Viridius said, "Save it."

She nodded. "To answer your question, the rest of The Outkast came to our defense. They captured Dro'ka and a few of his remaining warriors."

"How did they know we needed help?" Viridius asked.

She shrugged.

Viridius said, "And our losses?"

"The rest of my men and almost all of Aksutamoon's are dead. Not very many wounded. These are some big, tough bastards."

"And our group?"

Her head lowered as she chewed her lower lip, then looked up. "I haven't found Trakuta, K'aro, or Aksutamoon, but I found Gius." Viridius peered over her shoulder at the spear sticking out of Gius's chest.

Fuck.

"Is he dead?"

"Will be shortly. He asked to see you."

Viridius walked up to Gius and stood over him. "Looks like you're done this time," Viridius said.

Blood trickled out of the corner of Gius's mouth. "So it would seem."

"Who's going to pay me now?" Viridius asked.

"Valentinian . . . sent me to find you, so he will be the one to pay you," he said as coughs shook his body.

"If I don't leave for Batopia," Viridius replied.

Gius's smile revealed his bloodstained teeth. "You'll stay. Not for the cause, but because we are paying you to kill the emperor, and you want to kill him more than I do. Don't you want to stop running?"

Viridius blinked a few times, trying to shed the eyelash that was bothering him. "Would be nice."

Gius's eyes flicked back and forth. "I can't see. I . . . I can't see." His voice took an anxious tone. "Viridius, are you there?"

Viridius knelt next to him and held his hand. "Ain't left you yet." A look of ease and comfort crossed Gius's face. He wanted to use the right words, but all that crossed his lips was a low guttural groan. "I'm s—"

More blood cascaded from his mouth as he squeezed Viridius's hand.

"Go easy, old friend," Viridius said.

Gius's eyes glazed over, and a bloody froth escaped his lips. His chest rose one last time, then stilled. His dull open eyes stared into the gray volcanic sky. Viridius got to his feet and watched the dead being dragged into separate piles. The humans were missing most of their limbs, their bodies covered in extensive bite marks. The smell of shit overwhelmed the senses.

Those untested in battle vomited where they stood. Flies buzzed around the dead horses and alpurlics scattered around the battlefield. Aa'tu limped up to them with a bandage around his forehead. Viridius noticed he was missing more patches of black hair along his arms and legs. His mount lay behind him, multiple spears in its flank.

"Good fight," he grunted, leaning against his broken spear shaft.

A warrior dressed in a studded bronze and black leather cuirass came to Aa'tu's side and snapped to attention. He placed his hand over his heart, then removed his helm. His mane was ebony with a white stripe running down the center, his body merle.

The white apurlic hair on top of his helm flowed in the breeze as the two warriors spoke in their native language. Nigol limped up to Viridius, knelt by Gius, and folded Gius's arms across his chest. He placed two gold Wolfryian coins over Gius's eyes and smiled.

Viridius listened to the conversation across from him and waited for Aa'tu to finish. He waved Nigol over and told him what he wanted to say. Nigol's head bobbed up and down as he did his best to understand their dialect and what they were saying.

"He is introducing the warrior in black as his son, Tro'ka, heir to their pride. His warriors were the ones who saved us," Nigol said.

Viridius shrugged and walked away. Corcundia followed behind him, keeping pace. "Why did you not thank them?"

"Because they rode to save the other beasts, not us. We're slaves, remember?"

The two reached the center of the battlefield, where the fighting had been the worst. Aksutamoon and Trakuta sat on a dead D'atu warrior, passing a bottle of Tears of Tramonia between them. Only a handful of Aksutamoon's men were left. They sat around him, nursing their wounds. Heads were missing bodies, bodies were missing arms and legs, and men's torsos were strewn about in a macabre scene. Trakuta smiled wide, opening a wide gash across his brow.

"You all right?" Viridius asked.

"I'll live. More than I can say for our men," Trakuta said with an exhausted sigh.

"Gius is dead," Viridius said.

Trakuta spat on the ground and lifted his wine flask. "Good luck to the gods. He was a testy one."

Aksutamoon stood up and extended his arm. "You fight well. Thank you for watching my back."

"I didn't. You fell anyway. I should have been faster," Viridius said.

Aksutamoon patted his arm and tilted his head back, roaring with laughter, the giblets on his neck, shaking. "You did better than my men." He glanced at the corpses and winked. "Much better."

A warrior climbed over a pile of bodies holding his side. Corcundia noticed K'aro immediately and ran to him. She hugged him around the neck, burying her head in his mane.

"How are you still alive?" she asked.

"The gods are kind," he chortled.

One of The Outkast healers wandered over and helped him lie down. One arrow was stuck in his side, the other deep in his shoulder. The healer and K'aro growled at each other. Bracing himself, he roared as the healer yanked both arrows out. He inspected their tips and then threw them into the ash before moving on to help the others.

"How bad?" Corcundia asked.

"Not bad. My armor is made well," K'aro said.

He smiled at her, then spotted Dro'ka across the field. Sprinting as fast as he could, K'aro reached him with only a few bounds. He snatched him by the neck and squeezed, trying to crush his larynx. Aa'tu grabbed K'aro by the mane and threw him to the ground. "You're a slave, K'aro. You can't kill him."

K'aro balled his fist and sprang at Aa'tu. Calmly, Aa'tu sidestepped him and wrapped K'aro around the neck with the inside of his elbow. The headlock took K'aro's breath away and knocked him unconscious. Aa'tu dropped him, pulled Dro'ka to his feet, and then dragged him away, snarling. Mounted on a blue alpurlic, Tro'ka galloped up and glanced down at Viridius.

"You're free to go," he growled.

"Oh, how kind of you. We were leaving anyway," Viridius said.

"Don't press your luck, slave," he purred, his eyes turning to slits and his ears flattening against his skull.

"Call me a slave again, and you won't be quite so elegant when I finish with you," Viridius said.

Corcundia elbowed him and bowed stiffly. "Thank you for rescuing us. We are in your debt," she said.

Muttering under his breath, Viridius said, "The hell I am."

Tro'ka tilted his head. "What was that, slave?"

"Nothing, honored host. We will be leaving," Corcundia said with a disarming smile.

"You can take K'aro with you. He's no use to us," Tro'ka said.

K'aro held his head as he came to and stared at Tro'ka with a sneer.

"I am freeing you from your duties. Travel well, K'aro, last of the D'atu," Tro'ka said.

"You're mistaken. I'm not the last of my pride."

Howls of agony could be heard from where The Outkast had dragged Dro'ka and the rest of the Runners. A body impaled on a long spear through the rectum exited through the warrior's mouth.Viridius watched a spray of blood project from the body, and soon after, the remaining Runners were in the same position.

With a chuckle, Tro'ka watched K'aro's face. "You are now."

Dro'ka was the last to be impaled. His eyes were swollen shut, and his broken arms flopped around at different angles by his side. The R'atu dragged him back to the center of the battlefield as he screeched and bit at them. Aa'tu viciously kicked him behind the knees, sending him to the ash. The other warriors circled around, roaring in joy. A warrior placed a spear smeared in alpurlic feces at Tro'ka's feet.

Tro'ka picked it up, wrinkled his muzzle, and then glanced at K'aro. "Now you better be going, shield brother. We have a shitty business to attend to," he growled.

Dro'ka saw the blade and growled at Tro'ka. "Give me a sword and let me die with honor."

Tro'ka slapped one of his warriors on the shoulder with a roar. "Honor? You're talking to an Outkast. We have no honor."

Viridius didn't watch the exchange as he procured some horses and helped everyone mount. A warrior shouldered him aside in excitement and joined the group circling Dro'ka. Corcundia watched Dro'ka howl in agony as they impaled him. After a moment, she shook her head, glanced at her bloody hands, then massaged her knuckles.

"All this death," she whispered to herself.

Viridius glanced at her without a word and then turned his horse around and rode off. Sitting in her saddle, she watched the R'atu begin to make small cuts on Dro'ka's body, causing him to wiggle as he continued to howl.

K'aro cantered up and asked, "Lady Corcundia, shall we ride?"

A drop of blood welled at the corner of her eye. She closed her fist, twisted it quickly, and snapped Dro'ka's neck twenty feet away. His head rolled forward on his chest, then stopped as the blood dripped from his incisors. The R'atu were silent as they turned their attention to her in disbelief.

"Enough. Revenge is not the answer; forgiveness is," Corcundia shouted.

Tro'ka and Aa'tu approached her cautiously from the crowd. "You are a Last Blood?" Tro'ka asked.

She smeared the bloody tear away with the palm of her hand. "I was once, yes. Now, I am all that's left."

"The wizards of your group helped us reach the safety of the Lava Lands," Aa'tu purred more to himself than her.

"Yes, and we were exterminated by Wolfryia for it."

Aa'tu nodded. "This, I know." He stepped closer to her, his shadow flowing over her. "I thank you for helping my pridesmen escape the slaughter. We number less than a thousand now, but if your kind hadn't helped, we would be far less," he purred in perfect Dellosian.

Corcundia nodded and cut her eyes at K'aro, who watched with mild amusement as Aa'tu stared at his paws for a few moments.

"Brothers of The Outkast . . . hear me!" Aa'tu turned around and roared, raising his spear into the air. "We have to repay a blood debt, one that the old warriors like myself remember. All of you remember the shield brothers who died holding the humans back during their purge. What the young warriors don't know is the Last Bloods stayed with those shield brothers, so our cubs could escape."

A few warriors who had survived that costly retreat were standing in the front rank. They nodded at Aa'tu and knelt. Aa'tu continued. "The young warriors here must pay it back." He pointed at Corcundia. "That's a Last Blood—the only one of her kind. Many of you don't know, but the elders in every tribe signed a pact. We promised that we would protect any and all Last Bloods should we ever see them again." Aa'tu paused. "Who will follow me?"

Corcundia whispered to K'aro, "What is he saying?"

K'aro shrugged and dismounted. He freed his blade and slammed it into the ash. Taking a knee in front of her horse, he said, "I, K'aro, last of the D'atu, will follow you into death."

The other warriors roared and raised their spears and shields high above their heads. In unison, they shouted, "We of the Ba will ride with you."

Individually, hundreds of Ba warriors made a mark on their forearms and drove their bloody sword tips into the ash. Riding up beside her, Viridius chuckled.

"Whenever you're ready, Highness of Fur. We have to get to Rebellium headquarters."

She shot him a grim look, unimpressed with his cynical comments. She raised her sword, swung it over her head, and pulled the reins of her horse. "On me!"

TO BE CONTINUED . . .

CPSIA information can be obtained
at www.ICGtesting.com
Printed in the USA
LVHW031627040221
678388LV00003B/503

9 781954 161092